Ra
ru
yo
famny or Kelpies, chooks, horses, sheep and a time-share Jack Russell. She is passionate about encouraging non-readers to read, as well as inspiring both farmers to consider regenerative agricultural practices and animal handlers to better understand their dogs and livestock. Rachael is the proud patron of Agfest, Tasmania's world-class agricultural field day run by Rural Youth volunteers.

Rachael's first novel, *Jillaroo*, published in 2002, was a bestseller and has become one of Australia's iconic works of fiction, inspiring other country women to contribute to the genre of contemporary rural literature. She has gone on to write three other bestselling novels and a collection of short stories. *Fifty Bales of Hay* is her first foray into erotica after being inspired by her very naughty farming friends and talk that spread like wildfire in her country district about a certain book that came in a shade of grey. Her new novel, *The Farmer's Wife*, is coming out in April 2013.

 rachaeltreasure.com

 Rachael Treasure

 @rachaeltreasure

Also by Rachael Treasure

Rachael Treasure

Fifty Bales of Hay

HarperCollins*Publishers*

For ordinary everyday goddesses like you and me

HarperCollins*Publishers*

First published in Australia in 2012
by HarperCollins*Publishers* Australia Pty Limited
ABN 36 009 913 517
harpercollins.com.au

HarperCollins*Publishers*
Level 13, 201 Elizabeth Street, Sydney NSW 2000, Australia
Unit D, 63 Apollo Drive, Rosedale, Auckland 0632, New Zealand
A 53, Sector 57, Noida, UP, India
77–85 Fulham Palace Road, London W6 8JB, United Kingdom
2 Bloor Street East, 20th floor, Toronto, Ontario M4W 1A8, Canada
195 Broadway, New York NY 10007, USA

National Library of Australia Cataloguing-in-Publication entry:

Treasure, Rachael.
    Fifty bales of hay / Rachael Treasure.
    ISBN: 978 0 7322 9765 7 (pbk.)
    ISBN: 978 1 4607 0015 0 (ebook)
A823.4

Cover design by Natalie Winter
Cover images by shutterstock.com
Author photograph by Kevin O'Daly
Typeset in Palatino by Kirby Jones
Printed and bound in Australia by Griffin Press
The papers used by HarperCollins in the manufacture of this book are a natural,
recyclable product made from wood grown in sustainable plantation forests.
The fibre source and manufacturing processes meet recognised international
environmental standards, and carry certification.

Hello dear reader,

Can I please take a moment to let you know in real life I am a nerd? I am more likely to be found in bed with a thesaurus than with an actual bloke, so I must stress ... these stories are **fiction***. Because of this I haven't bored the reader with all the safe sex practices needed to get you through life to a healthy age without your private bits falling off. Therefore, I stress, to young and old, in real life practise safe sex and while you are at it, practise love, respect and kindness with the one you're with!*

Remember, no balloon, no party.

Rachael

Contents

Harvest Moon

*I*t was the sort of summer's day where the horizon took on liquid form and shimmered like clear moving jelly in the distance. It was the type of day that the red dirt of the road felt so hot that it might suddenly ignite into flames beneath the soles of one's boots.

And there was Stella in that sweltering heat, standing before her oven. It was the day of her tenth wedding anniversary. A decade ago, her mother-in-law-to-be had warned her not to get married around harvest time, but since she was a little girl, Stella had always wanted a summer wedding, so the January date was set. Should she have listened?

She swiped a sticky, persistent fly away from her face and blew her breath upwards to her dark fringe, trying to cool away the strand of hair that stuck to her brow. Standing in front of the fan-forced oven wearing only her wonky underwire bra and rather saggy black undies, Stella wondered why on earth the men needed cake for afternoon smoko on a day like today? Wouldn't a packet of shortbread biscuits do?

3

She sighed and felt a drip of sweat trickle down the small of her back. It wasn't so much her husband, Tom, nor his father, Dennis, demanding the tucker. Rather, the pressure came from her mother-in-law, the sort of pressure made by the unseen slow-moving push of boulders. Nancy was a perfectionist in everything on the home front, and particularly when it came to providing meals, which she dished up with a somewhat bitter pride. Nancy was especially upright in her body language when she delivered her signature smokos during harvest time or shearing. But it was the way Nancy wielded her love for her family and her control that had them swimming circles around her. She used her command of the home and the food as power over the men, and power over Stella. Her smiles were thinly disguised grimaces of a woman jaded by life.

'They work such long hours,' Nancy would tut-tut as she eyed Stella's sloppily folded washing piles, 'so they need their bellies fuelled with good home-cooked meals. None of that bought stuff. That won't feed a man. Packet cake and frozen shop-bought sausage rolls are cheating in my view. But that's just my view. You do what you like.'

The men worked such long hours? Yeah, sure, Stella thought. Long hours spent in the air-conditioned cabs of fancy tractors. Cabs that had stereos that broadcast the cricket all day, or iPod playlists of favourite country music. Then there was the social element of tractor driving, where the radio handpiece was a link to their mates harvesting grain in the district, always nearby. And they had the built-in drink holders, and the plug-in space for Eskys containing cold stubbies of beer when the long arm of the clock slipped past five o'clock. All this along with GPS controls so the men barely had to steer to get their grain rows straight. They only had to get out into the heat occasionally to adjust the chaser bin, open a gate, refuel or set up the grain auger. And then there were the trips to the railside grain weighbridge and silos. Sure it was routine, round the clock, hectic work … but it was mostly air-conditioned and social. Not like this kitchen. And there was no need for fancy smokos. No need at all.

The reason Stella knew all this and Nancy did not was because once, years ago, before the wedding, before the babies, Stella had been part of that tractor driving world. And she had loved it. It was before life crept up on her and took her to a place she never thought she would be. In a kitchen, while her beloved rural world moved on outside without her. Not for one moment did she begrudge her kids. But she missed being with Tom in *his* world. Instead, she was groomed by Nancy to become one of the 'womenfolk'. It depressed her.

Stella glanced at her goddess, sticky-taped to the fridge.

'Please help me today,' Stella said, looking at the image of Nigella Lawson standing in her British kitchen, curving wildly and womanly in a red dress that clung to ginormous knockers. Her white, full breasts brushed by the ends of her flowing dark hair. 'Please give me strength, Nigella,' Stella said again.

Tom had given her a Nigella cookbook last Christmas. She was certain Tom wasn't attracted to it for the recipes …

more for the fact that Nigella had pouting cherry lips and did things to strawberries and cream with her mouth that reminded him of fellatio. But Stella didn't care. She admired the woman. A woman who had suffered the death of loved ones. A woman who made cooking about love and sensuality, and about self-soothing. A woman who was comfortable with her curves and in the dead of night liked to stroke the shelves of her pantry and feast on midnight snacks. Nigella, in Stella's book, was a legend.

Stella wondered if Nigella had the same trouble with men, or did they treat her like the goddess she was? Did the men in Nigella's house do the dishes and bring her champagne, or cups of tea when reclining in the bath? Or when Nigella's men knocked off work, did they kick boots off at the back door to be tripped over, and after a quick wash, was the couch located and feet put up on stools and the television flicked on and the newspaper unfolded, and did the news or the sport become the focus? Not the kids. Not the wife. Not the domestics. Was it the same the world over?

If only they had a bath in this dump of a cottage, Stella thought, she could soak in it and Tom could bring her a Bundy. If only they had a *pantry* so she could soothe herself with some shelf stroking and learn to love her kitchen and her cooking the way Nigella did. Still, she reasoned, Nigella would certainly do more hours than the men. There was no doubt there. She was a mother.

For Stella, her day usually started at 5.30 a.m. with Ned's first bottle, and it wasn't done until she fell into bed in an exhausted heap after a hectic routine of domestic tasks and helping the men. There was the endless round of dirty dishes, bathing the kids, looking after the kids, planning the next day's meals, getting the washing away, sweeping the spiders from the verandah and watering the garden. Then there was helping the men working on the farm … round and round it went, on and on. To add to the pressure, there was the straightening of the cushions and curtains in case Nancy popped by, or hiding the twelve bucks' worth of 'naughty grey book' Tom had bought from the local truck stop in the hope it 'might get Stella horny so she would give him a bit'. She sighed. Couldn't Tom see she was just too tired to give him a bit? Her mind was too full of the daily grind of living. Bloody men.

But, Stella reasoned, with a steamy-breathed hot, hot sigh, Tom was a good bloke. Tom did his best. Considering the way Nancy had raised him, he really did try for her. He sometimes offered help with the barbecue or the dishes. And he often gave her cuddles at the sink when she was about to cry. But most of the time Tom was too busy for her. Preoccupied with the farm bookwork, or the internet — checking grain futures trading, scanning weather forecasts, dealing with emails, answering his mother's calls on the two-way from the homestead only a hundred metres away. His stress about 'providing for them as a family' knotting him into silence and distance at night. The busyness of the day sending them to bed at different times, both overwhelmed by their life.

But after ten years, they were still a team, thought Stella. He was still her man. He stood by her, through thick and thin. She wanted to be a good woman to him too, after all this time. Stella knew, as she looked around the tiny shoebox farm cottage that had no air-conditioning, only ceiling fans that whirred very fast as if they would take the house high up into the blue, they were both striving together for a better life. A home for themselves soon, on a second property. And who was she to complain? Tom's mother had raised five children in this same tiny farm cottage, before Dennis's parents had moved out of the big homestead to a retirement house in town. So, Stella thought, all she had to do was bide her time. For now, if the men wanted cake, they should have their cake. The only trouble was, after her tractor shifts ten years ago, she knew it was really only Nancy who wanted the cake. The men were happy with beer.

She grabbed up her oven mitts just as little Ned, unable to sleep in this afternoon heat and too tired to reason with, screamed from his cot. His face and chubby limbs blotchy and red, his bottle cast on the floor, the milk already curdling. The fan that whirred cooler air through Tom and Stella's bedroom was angled at his cot, but it seemed to make no difference to him, poor little man. Stella pouted to herself. The heat was bad enough for big people, let alone cherubic little Ned, who was such a good doer. He would be cooking in the tiny room that stood to the west of the house where the sun hung outside in a fiery blaze.

'Mummy's coming, sweetie! I just have to get the cake out of the oven. Please be patient.'

Ned was, as of last week, two years old, but Stella had never talked down to her children as if they were 'just babies'. She'd approached motherhood with the same philosophies she had used to train her working dogs when she was outback with her first job as a young ringer. She had learned from the stockmen that kids were like dogs: they needed plenty of praise, plenty of respect, loads of confidence building, but if they crossed the line and put themselves in danger, or busted out of a boundary, *snap.* Stella, the alpha bitch, would swoop, suddenly, with the conviction of a good strong leader, but with no malice. Then all would be forgiven, the praise returning, the equilibrium found. As a result, her kids and her dogs were happy and confident, but also, when needed, they knew how to behave. She was proud of them. Her dogs and her kids. And she found times when she was proud of herself. Then Nancy would come calling and she would feel like the worst mother in the world.

She thought of her poor darling Milly who would be on the school bus, melting along with her bedraggled, sagging classmates. Just the idea of getting in the ute and sitting on the cracked, roasting vinyl seats to make the drive to the highway to meet the bus made Stella sag herself. She'd have to take Ned today. She couldn't just leave him. Sometimes she could risk it for half an hour, while he was down for his afternoon sleep, but not today. A renewed wave of screaming from Ned travelled through the narrow hallway and met her thoughts in the kitchen.

'Seen and not heard,' Nancy would mutter on the matter of children. 'In my day, when I was raising Tom and the other children …' Blah, blah, blah, thought Stella.

In Nancy's day, love was withheld for the sake of discipline. Not now, Stella thought. Times had changed. What would Nancy know about shaping young minds? Nancy had never worked a dog, never trained a pup. She had never had to reach deep within to look at how her own inner self played out in the physical world of communicating with creatures as sensitive as sheep, as cunning as cattle and as clever as dogs. What would Nancy think if she knew the principles of working-dog handling were also applied by Stella to the management of her husband, Tom? Stella smiled.

At times, Tom was as sharp and energetic as a kelpie, other times as dopey and lovable as a Labrador. All he basically needed was a good feed, plenty of praise and the occasional hump to keep him happy. But that was the sticking point. The hump. Stella had felt a slow corrosion take hold in the area of their lovemaking. It was the one area where her marriage felt as if it was fully weighted down with the burdens of life. Where was there room for it amongst the dirty washing, the crops to sow, grow and harvest, sheets to change, floors to sweep and mop, head lice to combat, lunchboxes to empty of sodden crusts and half-sucked oranges, mouldy scraps to toss to the chooks, soiled nappies to shove in the already smelly wheelie bin ...

Where was the spark in their marriage? Where was that girl who had craved her man? She had dissolved and, like a mirage on the horizon, the more Stella chased her in her mind, the more the girl evaporated when she neared.

She thought about the early years of their courtship. The first year of harvest when she had stayed on the farm in the big house. Nancy had handed her the smoko basket and showed her on the farm map which of the right-angled roads to turn down to find the paddock where Tom was harvesting. Gleefully Stella had lobbed into the clunky farm ute, started it up and raced down the driveway.

That was back when the old yellow New Holland harvester was still going. Tom and Stella were three months into their relationship. She could see Tom in the header, the combs gobbling up the golden wheat that pushed out in front of the roaring machine, the auger spurting full-yielding seed heads into the bin towed behind the combine. She couldn't wait to get to him. He'd barely slowed the vehicle and she'd sprung up onto the step and climbed into the cab. Without a word, they'd greeted each other with a passionate kiss. Sitting on the hydraulic sprung seat, she'd dragged her shorts off, tugged down his, and impaled herself hungrily on the hardness of his waiting shaft while the idling harvester roared in her ears. Later, Nancy was curt with them. Tom hadn't eaten his angel cake. Stella had giggled and Tom had suppressed a smile. He sure had eaten Stella's angel cake, he'd said later to Stella wickedly. But that was years ago now. Those days, long gone.

Stella opened the oven door and a blast of heat escaped to further thicken the air of the room. She swiped a strand of her jet-black hair from her eyes and stooped, with oven mitts on, to look at the chocolate cake within. The cake sagged in the middle.

'It's all very well for you, Nigella,' she said. 'You poms don't have to deal with the fucking flies, and heat like this, and I bet you don't have a mother-in-law like mine!'

As Ned cried out again, and Stella bent to retrieve the cake that resembled a sunken cowpat, she burnt her wrist on the oven and swore.

'Fuck meee!' she said, flicking her arm in pain.

'If you like,' came a voice behind her. Tom was standing there in his shorts and a blue singlet. He came up behind her and grabbed her by the hips. 'Even in those undies, I would.'

'Oh, for god's sake, Tom!' she said, juggling the hot cake tin, her wrist stinging and already rising in a red welt. 'Can't you hear Ned chucking a spaz? I've just fucking burnt myself and I've got to get Milly off the bus!'

'Dressed like that? Old Trev will have a heart attack and crash the school bus.'

She pulled a face at him and frowned. 'Why aren't you harvesting?' she said, dumping the cake and going to their bedroom to get Ned from his cot. The poor child felt like a steamed dim sim.

'Too hot!' shouted Tom from the kitchen. 'Dad called it off for the rest of the arvo. Likely to start a fire with the machinery.'

'Here,' she said, passing Ned to Tom and filling up a sipper cup of water at the sink. 'Can you mind him for a bit while I get Milly?' She passed Tom the cup.

Tom made an apologetic face. 'Dad wants me to go get parts.'

'Well, why not meet the bus and take Milly with you to get the parts?' she asked, a little impatiently.

Tom shook his head. 'Poor Milly! It's too hot for a trip back into town with her and you know it. Tell you what, I'll wait with Ned. You go get her.'

'Fine,' said Stella, wincing as she ran her burnt hand under the tap.

'Before you put your clothes back on, you know … could we?' Tom said, waggling his dark eyebrows up and down, his eyes hopeful. 'We can plonk Ned in front of the telly for two minutes. You know. An anniversary bonk? Just a quickie.'

Stella glanced at the clock. 'Now? C'mon, Tom. There isn't time.'

'I know,' he said sullenly. He planted a kiss on Stella's sweat-covered forehead and took Ned with him into the tiny office, which was more like a cupboard. She heard him boot up the computer. She pulled on her sundress, shoved on her work boots and went out into the blistering heat to fetch Milly.

'Welcome to my world, Nigella, welcome to my world!'

Stella had just set the steak out on the kitchen bench when the radio came to life. 'Stella, you on channel?'

It was Tom. He delivered the news over the crackle of the two-way for Nancy in the homestead to hear too. News that they would harvest through until late, now the day had cooled a little. News that he wouldn't be back till after ten that night.

'And by the way, happy anniversary, babe. Over,' he said. Stella hung up the radio handpiece, put the steaks back in the fridge, reached into the freezer to dig out two lemonade icy poles and thrust them at Milly and Ned. Then she flicked on the TV to ABC kids.

'Watch him for me for a bit, please, Milly,' she said. 'Thanks, darling. Mummy needs a ten-minute power nap.'

Milly, perplexed by the sudden arrival of icy poles just before tea, nodded her little dark curly head at her mother and proceeded to open the treat for her little brother first, then herself. Stella shut the door of her bedroom, sat down on the bed and began to cry. She slid open the top drawer of the bedside table and pulled out the gift she had ordered for Tom. She undid the lid and as she did, smeared the tears away over her sweating hot face.

She had saved every cent for this anniversary gift for Tom. Money that she had made from selling two litters of kelpie pups she had bred. Her plan this evening had been to cook Tom up a big steak, have a beer with him once the kids were in bed, put on the new lingerie she'd ordered off the net, then give him his present. Then give him herself.

Inside the beautiful timber box was a thick leather belt, made by the local saddler, but what was most stunning about the belt was the buckle.

Stella, their tenth anniversary in mind, had a few months ago ventured round the back of the machinery shed where her husband's old busted-up 1980 Holden WB Statesman sat slumped, wheel-less and rusting, on blocks beneath a pepper tree. The ute was just a body now, stripped of its engine, the three panels including the roof still dented from the night Tom had rolled it coming back with Stella from a B&S ball. He hadn't been over the limit. Tom was reliable like that. Once they knew neither of them weren't seriously injured, they had joked that the dopey roo they had hit on the slippery gravel road must've been drinking, the way it had suddenly wobbled in front of them.

But she had felt Tom's sadness when the mechanic had told them the ute was a write-off. His hurt was tangible. He loved that ute. She loved that ute. It was a link to the days when their love had first begun to bloom.

With a screwdriver and a small hammer, Stella had carefully chipped off the metal steering-wheel badge. The badge was silver and held the logo of the proud Holden lion that sat with its paw on a globe. She had rubbed the badge on her jeans as she walked back home, then set the collector's metal disc on the kitchen table and carefully and intricately sketched her design around it. It had cost her fifty bucks to ship the thing to the States, but the craftsman there had done a brilliant job of setting the ute badge into a rodeo-size buckle with the wording *1980 WB Statesman* amid looped swirls and entwined ropes of silver and gold. On the back, in fancy steel writing, he had inscribed: *Happy 10th anniversary, Tom. Eternal love, Stella.*

Stella ran a fingertip over the tiny bumps and curves of the beautiful buckle. Then she put the lid on the box, threw the lingerie that was still in the postage bag into the cupboard and put the lid on her plans for a romantic evening with her man. Then she closed the door on her feelings. She had kids to feed and get to bed.

A little later, Stella fell asleep beneath the whir of the fan and didn't even wake when, around eleven, Tom crept into the room, stripped off to his jocks and, still covered in a film of grain dust, fell into bed beside her. Too hot for sheets, he lay there and looked at the whirring fan in the darkness, glanced at the baby snoring softly in his cot, and patted Stella gently on her hot, clammy thigh.

'Sorry, honey. Sorry.' Within minutes, he too was asleep.

Stella sat up suddenly in surprise.

'Tom?' she said, a frown on her face, fear sliding into her voice. Outside the window was a bright orange glow. A fire? she wondered in shock. She slid her hand to Tom's side of the bed, but the rumpled sheets were cool and he was not there. She looked to Ned, who was lying on his stomach, his little sumo-legs sprawled out, his arms cast wide, sound asleep. Stella ran from the bedroom and banged through the flyscreen door and came to a standstill on the verandah.

With a gasp, she felt a rush within her. There was no fire. There was no danger. What had woken her was the most beautiful, glowing ball of the biggest harvest moon she had ever seen in her life. It was full and red and round, burning and moving in a swirling, giant orange-golden orb. The moon was sitting low against the horizon and shone out across the dam as if it too was transfixed by its beautiful reflection there. At the heart of the dam, Stella noticed ripples on the surface. In the moonlight, she could see Tom swimming. His big, tanned farmer's arms flinging over in the water, tumble-turning, floating on his back. Stella smiled at the sight.

She crept back inside the house. She opened up the cupboard, took out the box and reached in for the parcel.

A few minutes later, Tom bobbed to the surface. Across the shimmering water, he saw his wife in the moonlight, slipping through the fence and walking down from the house. She was wearing her best cowgirl boots and a black lace corset that pushed her full breasts high and together so they were rounded up to perfection. She had her long dark hair woven up and she was carrying two beers and a box with a silver ribbon that glinted in the moonlight. She came to stand by the dam bank, her legs spread a little apart, cowgirl tough, cowgirl beautiful, the moonlight washing along the smooth tapering muscles of her thighs. In the water, naked, Tom felt an erection stir.

'Happy anniversary,' she called. 'Just. It's three minutes till midnight.'

Tom grinned and swam to her. Dripping wet, he tottered over the rubble of dam-side rocks and clay and came to stand next to her in the pasture.

'What are you up to, honey?' she said.

'I couldn't sleep. Too hot. Needed to cool off.'

'Here,' Stella said, passing him an ice-cold beer.

'Oh! You are my dream woman, Stella! And you look hot. So hot.' He took the beer, chinked the neck of the stubby on hers and swigged. They drank in silence together, him holding her from behind, still dripping with dam water, desire casting his penis erect.

'Have you ever seen a moon like it?' Stella said, leaning back into the cool wetness of his naked body and nuzzling her head against his chest.

'Uh-uh. Never,' Tom said. They both stood before the moon, close, their breath falling in line with each other's. The giant yellow disc seemed larger than planet Earth. The heat of the landscape caused it to shimmer at its base and it was encircled by a ring of soft white light.

'Amazing,' Stella said. 'Makes you suddenly wake up to yourself and think none of it matters really. None of it. The harvest. The washing. The cooking. The rush. Only the people you love matter.'

Tom smiled and gently rubbed his hand on her tight neck. 'You matter to me. So much. I love you, Stella.' She looked down, feeling almost shy in the moment, a soft smile on her pretty pink mouth.

He set his beer down, turned her around, then pulled her to him, stooping to kiss her and fold her into his arms. Kissing with love, kissing with passion before the giant harvest moon.

She inclined her mouth invitingly up to his and gasped at the sensuous feeling of his torso pressed against hers. She felt the desires of her body, dormant for so long, rush to life. It was like a spark fused in her brain. Her body drinking in all that she could as she began to kiss her husband with a fierce wanting. Her husband of ten years, a love that had sprung from B&S balls, from Bundaberg Rum and wild circle work in utes, and lazy Saturdays spent lying by rivers. A love sprung from bed sheets rumpled in passionate lovemaking, of laughter rising up from quickies had in hay sheds, on tractors and on the backs of utes when the olds were away. Their history shared, their young country love now rejoined and renewed, the moon as their witness.

Stella felt her husband's hands roam further downwards towards the wetness between her legs. His erection was pressing urgently against her thigh. She wanted to prolong the moment, so she pulled away. This moon, this night, was a gift. She wanted to savour it. To tempt her man. To tease him. So that when he had her, she was the prize he had so longed to win.

'Wait. I have something for you.' She passed the gift to him. Tom opened the box and his jaw dropped when he saw what lay within. The buckle reflecting its silver and gold beauty back to the moonlight. She encouraged him to turn it over and as he read the inscription, she saw emotion well in his eyes.

He pulled Stella to him and buried his face into her neck. 'Oh, thank you, baby. It's brilliant. I love you. So much. Happy tenth anniversary too, babe.' He held her hand and turned towards the moon. 'You know, somewhere out in the future when we are old and grey and have grandkids asking to borrow my belt buckle, drink my beer and use my grandpa car, I'll be saying to you "Happy *fiftieth* anniversary, Stella darling". Because I know right at this moment, I'm goin' to love you forever. You're my woman.'

Stella's expression gave way to tears as she looked into the face of the moon and then looked at the beautiful face of her man. In her heart, she knew what Tom said was true. They would love forever. Eternally.

She kicked off her boots and turned so Tom could unhook the eyelets of her corset. She folded the garment away from her body, dropping it onto the bleached summertime grasses, revealing her naked body to him. Then she turned to her man and put her arms about his neck. He scooped her up and carried her into the dam. The water lapped at their limbs as they tumbled into the wash of cool brown water, the slide of mud between their toes washed clean with each kick. Together they swam to the middle where the moon pooled in a big yellow melted disc at the dam's heart. There they kissed, like first-time lovers, deeply, gently, lingeringly, until every nerve ending of each other's body was alive, almost glowing with electric energies. Entwined, limbs sliding over one another, Tom found footing on a long forgotten boulder and also found his place deep within his wife, sliding her body onto his cock. With relief, he simply held her there, conjoined, both of them drinking in the closeness. As they began to gently move in slow, deeply penetrating pulses, Stella kissed the water from her husband's hot skin. He tasted of soils, rich with life. He tasted of farm life and of love. And there under the wash of the moon, Stella joined the stars as she cried out with the climax of her life clutching her deep within. Her husband, Tom, journeyed with her and together they both drifted into the ether in a love renewed.

* * *

The next morning, Stella woke to the sound of Ned burbling, 'Mum, mum, mum, mum,' in his cot beside the bed. Tom was nowhere to be found on the rumpled, sweat-sagging sheets that spoke of restless hot harvest nights. He was long gone to work. She dragged herself up, pulling on Tom's T-shirt, feeling a strange rush of desire merely from the lingering scent of him on the garment. She remembered the moon. Was it all a dream?

Sleepily she stood. 'I'll get you a bottle, mate,' she said to her boy and groggily she made her way out to the kitchen, glancing in on Milly who was still deeply asleep in her little girl's bed. Still half asleep herself, Stella stood at the kitchen bench and glanced at the picture of Nigella on the fridge.

'Well? Did I dream it?'

Nigella said nothing, but she seemed to be looking in the direction of the laundry. As the kettle bubbled steam into the already warm morning air, Stella glanced into the laundry. On the floor lay a crumpled pile of clothing, along with Tom's work shorts, her old bra. Also on the pile was a fine, black lace corset, crusted with dam clay.

Stella smiled to herself. She turned back to the kitchen where she saw the gifted belt buckle propped up in its box, sitting in pride of place in the centre of the table. There was also a note.

No need to cook smoko for me, darling. I'll be in at ten-thirty to eat you instead, baby! Your loving (sexy) husband of ten happy years, Tom xx

Stella held the note to her heart and turned to face the fridge.

'You did this, didn't you, Nigella? You gave us the moon last night.' She smiled with tears in her eyes and began to laugh at her good fortune, and as she did, she was sure she saw her goddess wink.

The Crutching

The handpiece vibrated in Mervyn Crank's strong grip as he dabbed the last bit of wool from the tail of a ewe and gently let her go. She slid in a stunned stupor with her little cloven feet cast in the air and disappeared down the chute to the count-out pens below the shearing shed. There she joined the other fifty Pine Hills ewes who, because they had the dirtiest tails, had been drafted off to be crutched and wigged a second time before lambing. The early spring flush of lush green grass and no access to dry tucker to bind them up a bit had been giving the ewes grief, and Mervyn Crank was not a man to allow a lamb to come into the world through a veil of sodden dung at a ewe's rear end. He'd been happy to help Mrs Taylor out with the crutching again.

Mervyn slipped out of the shearer's backsaver sling that hung from the rafters of the shearing shed. The sling creaked a little on its taut spring as it dangled and bounced in the warm evening air. Sweat had beaded on Mervyn's lined brow and pooled in his tufted grey eyebrows. He flexed backwards, placing two big hands into the small of his back, and groaned a little as he arched his tired muscles.

'She was the one I've been looking for today,' Mervyn said, grabbing up his water cooler. 'The last one!' He took a swig. 'Getting too old for this game. I only crutched fifty and look at me!'

Mrs Taylor, who had been watching him in silence for the past fifteen minutes, stepped forward, unhooked his towel hanging from the nail near the shearer's stand and handed it to him. He took it with an inclination of his head and a glance of gratitude in his vibrant light blue eyes. As he swiped the towel across his face, he winked at Mrs Taylor and said, 'Thank you, madam.'

She indicated the clock on the wall. 'Yes, tired you may be, but you completed the task in good time,' she said in a smooth and gentle voice. 'You'll make your first of the season lawn bowls competition with time to spare, of that I am certain.' Mrs Taylor slipped her elegant hand into the pocket of her black mohair cardigan. 'How much do I owe you, Mervyn?'

Mervyn looked at the red lipstick applied perfectly to Mrs Taylor's lined but still full and shapely mouth, then lifted his gaze to her large, hooded brown eyes. Her eyes were clouded with what seemed like a lifetime's sadness mixing and melting into two pretty dark pools. In her younger days, she'd been a stunner around town, a dead ringer for Audrey Hepburn. She still was in a way. Mervyn tapped his fingertips on his lips as he thought, his eyes fixed on hers. She didn't belong here. Not here in the shed, and not here in this district. She was graceful and nervous, like a deer, but those who knew deer knew that they were also strong and elusive creatures. And like a deer, Mrs Taylor's line, the shape her body made in the world, was utterly smooth and beautiful, like one of the china figurines his Sheila used to order from the magazines for her cabinet. Mervyn stopped his finger tapping.

'I reckon fifty bucks oughta do it, Mrs Taylor,' Mervyn said.

Mrs Taylor shifted her sparrow-like weight in her little red flats on the board and pulled the cardigan of her twin-set about her bony shoulders. She frowned at him, fingering invisible pearls. Mervyn couldn't help notice a button missing on the cardigan that was pilling under the sleeves a little. He noticed there was a small hole in the shoulder of the garment. The signature pearl necklace parodied by everyone around the district was missing too. He watched as Mrs Taylor tried to swallow her pride, but still she shook her head. 'No, Mervyn. I owe you more.' Mrs Taylor held two golden fifty-dollar notes in her slim piano-concerto player's fingers. She unfolded them and offered them up to Mervyn. Her deerlike eyes were on him, pleading for him to take the money.

He sighed, scratched the back of his head, then with kindness in his eyes, plucked only one note from her.

'There was just a handful to crutch out of the whole mob. It's no problem.' He cast his eyes to the floor where a scattering of dags lay. 'And it'll take me no time to tidy up.'

'I'll pay you what's due,' she said curtly. 'I don't want your charity. And I certainly don't want anybody's pity.'

Mervyn smiled. It was so like her. The impenetrable veneer of the grazier's wife. Rural royalty.

Picking up the wool paddle, he began to draw the dags into a pile, glancing at her, his eyes crinkling at the sides.

'Who says charity and pity are what I'm giving you, Mrs Taylor? Maybe I like coming here,' Mervyn said quietly. 'Maybe I'd like to give you something other than that. If you catch my drift.'

Mrs Taylor's eyes darted to him, one perfectly shaped and pencilled eyebrow arching up at him in surprise. He turned his back and with his strong crutcher's hands, he grasped two short wooden planks and stooped down, using them to scoop up the dags and toss them into the bin. Then he turned to sort the few crutchings on the wool table, flicking them into two piles of dirty and clean wool. The striped belt that he wore about his waist held his shearer's dungarees neatly at his waist. He was fit for a man of his age, and Mrs Taylor had spent the afternoon admiring this aspect of him. He had a steady patience with the ewes should any get testy and start beating their hind legs violently against the floor as he crutched. And brawny though he was, he had a gentlemanly quality about him, even when handling the sheep and dogs out in the yards.

Mrs Taylor stood now on the board feeling her pulse flutter in her throat like a butterfly caught against glass. How long had it been? she wondered. How long? She took in his broad shoulders that were stooped a little from age, but his character remained upright. He was a good man, Mervyn. Decent and clean. Kind and mild. Mrs Taylor liked that.

When she had first climbed the steep steps into the shearing shed, the pain from her arthritic knees had dissolved when she had caught sight of Mervyn bent over the sheep, intent on his work, held in a shaft of light from the skylights, more golden and serene than the light that spilled into cathedrals through stained glass, and the buzz of the handpiece delivering up a meditative drone. The peace of the place and the presence of Mervyn working with the animals had soothed Mrs Taylor instantly.

Mrs Taylor had felt a rush through her body at the sight of the quiet man at toil. There was a sense of gratitude within her, but she recognised something else. What she had felt was a rush of desire. And a surge of love for this man. Mervyn had been the one, through thick and thin, who had been there for her, in the background, since her husband had died. He was the reason she had remained here on Pine Hills.

Mrs Taylor had watched Mervyn for a while without his awareness of her presence. She saw that he moved like a dancer. The way he glided the handpiece around the ears of the ewes and across their pretty, startled faces, shearing the tips of the grey wool away to reveal divine white fibres. The way he gently let the creatures down the drop after the wigging and crutching and, unfurling himself from the sling, moved to the catching pen to grab up another one.

As he dragged a ewe backwards and again manoeuvred himself into the sling, he had seen Mrs Taylor standing there. He knew he had been caught unguarded. She had witnessed his surprised look, quickly followed by a gentle smile of genuine gladness that she was before him. She had felt the rush then. She felt the rush now.

'What are you offering to give me other than that, Mervyn?' Her voice was soft. Informal. Not the voice she used with the farm workers or people of the town. With his back to her, Mervyn stopped sorting the crutchings and stood very still.

'I get lonely too, since Sheila passed,' he said. 'I know what it's like. I was thinking of giving you some company.'

He turned, and Mrs Taylor saw the look of longing in his eyes.

'I like seeing you. You are very easy on the eye, Mrs Taylor,' Mervyn said, looking sincerely at her. 'But it's not just your beauty. It's just … you. You. I very much enjoy the company of you.'

Mrs Taylor sucked in a breath and her hand flew to her throat where the butterfly wings were beating hard, as if in death throes. She felt the absence of the protective string of pearls, which had been pawned in the city. None of the shed staff would *ever* have talked to her like that in her husband's day, she thought. Never! Mind you, she would never have ventured to the shed. She would have been more likely to be found in the giant homestead arranging flowers, or typing CWA meeting minutes, or sinking hopelessly into an early glass of brandy and dry before the children arrived home from boarding school.

In her prime, Mrs Taylor was the most loathed grazier's wife in the district. She kept the other women on their toes with her perfect clothing, her string of quality Japanese pearls (harvested in the War years) and with her hated dance lessons in the local hall. The classes were executed with regimental strictness for the benefit of the uncultured and often overweight local girls. To top it all off, Mrs Taylor had been a beauty and a homemaker in that unreachable, perfect way.

Little did the people in the district know that her husband, crafty old Mr Taylor, who had a fetish for young dancing girls, had actually discovered Mrs Taylor in a questionable hotel in Sydney's Kings Cross. Back then, she was Elsie Morgan.

Old Mr Taylor had found Elsie during what had been a dark time for her. Elsie had been a showgirl working in scant costumes fashioned from cheap satin and golden tassels. In a room, under the harsh shine of a spotlight, with a backdrop of red velour curtains, Elsie had worked most nights doing her 'tease and trapeze' act. The ropes of her trapeze were entwined with faux flowers and the air was woven with the dark thoughts of the desperate men who shuffled in to sit in surly shadows and watch her. There on the stage, in the air, she would contort and writhe in her revealing clothing for the men, for the money for her rent or, occasionally, for an abortion. Her dreams of Broadway and acting slowly dissipated as yet another man, such as Mr Taylor, ran his hands along the milky white of her impossibly young and soft inner thighs and found her wet weakness.

Fixated, Mr Taylor had visited Elsie again and again at the hotel, and not long after the Sydney Royal Easter Show he had brought her home as his wife, pregnant at seventeen. He the older gentleman farmer; she the young wife with a questionable past and a desire to escape what she had known.

Her history had been discreetly buried with old money and a fake pastoral pedigree linking her to the west. Her time in the city with men had made her a clever actress, and she fell into her role of grazier's wife easily, at least on the exterior. In a short time, after her first baby, Giles, was born, followed quickly by Sophia, Mrs Taylor was accustomed to pretending that she was a good and graceful countrywoman. In the same way, her husband pretended to be a good farmer and a good husband. But Mrs Taylor knew never to trust him. Never to trust men.

And she had been right. The day after Mr Taylor died, the solicitor came calling. Mr Snell had stood before her in a rather has-been suit with a look of smugness, barely disguised, on his face. Mr Snell happily told Mrs Taylor that her husband had left her with a massive farm debt and a farm about to fold. Of course, Giles was of no use away in London and, naturally, Sophia wanted the property sold to provide money for her and her husband's renovations in Double Bay and to pay for the grandchildren's university education. But Mrs Taylor had held strong against her spoiled children and grandchildren, like an icy glacier. She made sure everything was very hard to do and that she and others moved very slowly. So far, five years on, the farm remained.

It was hard for her to believe it was five years since Mr Taylor had left her with the debt. Mrs Taylor had managed to not just hang on, but to begin to find herself again after all these frozen years.

With the help of Merv, and Timothy the jackaroo, she had kept Pine Hills ticking over and had kept the greedy children at bay. Mrs Taylor knew she had to be a strong woman. Very strong. But now, here in the shed, she had keenly felt the loneliness that had seeped into her bones. She wanted to spend the last years of her life knowing that there were kind men out there in the world. Men who could be trusted. Men who admired women deeply, but with a purity of their souls. Not the way the men were in that hotel years ago; not the way Mr Taylor had treated her, as if she was another one of his items of property. A tool that functioned to smooth his way through life and lift his status. A commodity.

Today, watching Mervyn in the beam of diffused light from the skylights in the shearing shed, she had felt the years falling away from her as she remembered her girlhood when she believed in a world of love and romance, a world where men had loving intentions and honour within. Now, with Mervyn Crank's soft voice and kind words, Mrs Taylor felt the stress tied up within her suddenly loosen, and there before Mervyn, she felt it unravel and tumble out. She swallowed as emotion crawled up her throat and clutched her there, the butterfly stilled. No breath coming. A choking. She felt her cheeks flame and the tears rise; she began to quiver and tremble.

Mervyn sensed her distress, saw her tears and the grappling for her throat. He moved over to her. Awkwardly at first, but then he cast his big strong arms around her. He felt her wiry, birdlike body fold into his chest, and as she gave into him, he released any apprehension and held her like he wanted to hold her. The embrace of a lover. The hug of a man who had desired her for the length of years.

Mrs Taylor felt it too. She lifted her head and suddenly she was kissing him. She felt the heaviness of his lips on hers and the urgent force of his torso pressed against her. She inhaled the masculine scent of him and felt herself waken. Then, as if life suddenly began again to tick over for her, Mrs Taylor felt herself breathe easily for the first time in years. She ran her hands down the front of his body and, beneath her delicate palms, she felt Mervyn's penis in his dungarees swell to life. Just the hardness, there, against her thigh, so very near her vagina, deepened her breath as if she was suddenly revived. How long had it been? *How long had it been?*

She inhaled deeply as she kissed him, the scent of him waking every cell in her body. Waking them from a dormancy spanning years. *Years.*

Suddenly Mrs Taylor was drawing off her cardigan, stepping out of her skirt and shedding her floral blouse. Suddenly she was Elsie. She stood before Mervyn Crank in her little red flats and black slip trimmed with lace. Goosebumps shimmered over her skin, despite the western country heat of the sleepy afternoon. She took Mervyn's hand, looked deeply into the safety of his eyes and delivered him the gaze of the showgirl. Elsie, the Broadway star. She lifted his hand slowly, fluidly above her head, then did a perfect pirouette, a girlish smile lighting her face, a distant youth coming alive in her sad eyes.

Before him she began to dance. Not the style of dance she taught the walrus-footed girls at the local hall, but the dances she *used to do*. The dances she had begun to practise again in the dead of her solitary nights in the time since her husband had gone. She flicked her leg lithely through the air, undulated her body this way and that, leaped towards Merv, brushing a beautiful hand around his neck, past his stubbled cheek and down to his chest. Then she danced away and slipped herself gracefully through the shearer's sling, inserting both feet through the gap and sitting her tiny bottom upon it as if it was a swing. She suggestively arched her body backwards, her breasts angled towards the skylights and her toes pointed ballet-perfect to the cobwebbed rafters of the shearing shed. When she swung back upright, her hair had loosened from its ivory clasp and was tumbling in silver waves against the angled bone of her shoulders.

'Come,' she said to Merv, who was standing in disbelief, desire raging in his pants.

He stepped forward and stood irresistibly close to her. With grace and determination, she unbuttoned his fly and slowly moved forward, where her mouth fell upon his cock. Hungrily she sucked from where she sat on the sling. He set his big hands on her slim shoulders and moaned as Mrs Taylor gently bounced, her mouth sliding up and down over the shaft of his penis. Her tongue circling its helmet-dome head. Next, Merv was reaching down, peeling away her pantyhose, pulling her pants down her legs. With the strength of ten men, he reefed on the rope and pulled the sling higher from where it was slung on the rafters, then guided Mrs Taylor to turn away from him. She lay on her stomach within the arc of the wool-covered sling that was marked with Merv's sweat. Her bottom, swathed in the satin of her slip, angled upwards to him.

He caressed her along her back, moving the sheeny fabric up and over her skin. When he heard her moan with desire, Merv slid his thick fingers in to find her wetness and stroked her clitoris. Mrs Taylor cried out, a deep, surprising cry. Then, unable to hold back any more, Merv gently eased into her from behind. Slowly at first, then with more intensity, he began to plunge in and out of her. The shearer's sling resisted each and every thrust and bounced them back together over and over again, the squeaking of the taut spring gaining a frantic rhythm. And then Mrs Taylor's pleasure came in waves, her back and head arched, her hands grappling behind her to grip the flesh of Merv's strong thighs. The sound of Mrs Taylor coming put Merv into a flush of desperation … it was too soon for it to end now, he had to have Mrs Taylor another way.

He guided Mrs Taylor to stand facing him so she viewed his glistening erection as he turned and sat in the sling. Then he invited her to straddle him, her sex gliding over his penis so that both of them gasped at once when they were joined, completely, deeply. The elasticity of the sling again gave them both lift and soon they were bouncing in perfect dancers' time, his cock driving upwards into her, she drawing downwards with her wetness. And then, as if singing opera to the gods, Mrs Taylor let go with a cry that set her dead husband's old dogs howling on their chains a kilometre away at the grand old Pine Hills homestead. Mervyn Crank followed suit, orgasming into her with a throaty howl.

When they had caught their breath and stepped off their private stage, Mervyn took Mrs Taylor's hand and on the shearing shed board, amid the bins of crutchings and the scent of fine merinos, Mervyn pulled her to him and began to guide her in a slow and beautiful waltz.

'I love you, Mrs Taylor,' he said, breathing in the gentle floral scent of her hair. 'No disrespect to my Sheila, but I always have and I always will.'

'Please,' Mrs Taylor said, 'call me Elsie. From now on, I am your Elsie.'

Droving Done

'*W*ell? You still wanna give it a go?' Kelly said, looking up at the long skinny stretch of a jackaroo standing before her.

She couldn't believe what she was about to do, let alone imagine what it would be like.

Wayne Carter, the jackaroo, had hips as thin as a greyhound, his torso was a long concertina of wide-spaced ribs, and his legs were lengthy enough to be used as upright posts in a hay shed. Old Snooza, the grader driver, reckoned the boy was so tall and thin you could swing him round above your head by his boots and crack the hat off him. No wonder the fellas on Bilga Station had given him the nickname Narra, a name that had stuck like dam-side clay.

It was only natural that Kelly and Narra were teamed up often for jobs, because Kelly had the nickname of Sparra, and it gave the staff on Bilga the opportunity for a great deal of mirth to have Narra and Sparra working together, one of them barely making five foot, the other nearly reaching seven. Kelly was the sort of pint-sized kid who had never grown and even in her mid-twenties still remained as tiny as a field mouse. When she had first

41

turned up in her Subaru ute for the job as a jillaroo on Bilga, the overseer had looked down at her. Frowning, he had said, 'What are you? Twelve?'

Snooza reckoned Sparra would fly away in a strong breeze and whenever he entered the jillaroo–jackaroo quarters, he'd call her name and pretend to seek her out under the couches. But as the team got to know her, Snooza reckoned Kelly was so big in spirit that she had more guts than an offal pit and more determination than a dog digging into a bitch's box. The blokes all liked her, including Narra, who stood before her now at the watering hole that was dotted with cow dung from a recently departed herd of cattle. Kelly tried to search for some eye contact with Narra to gauge if he was still willing. She had to crane her head right back to search his expression because it was hidden under a broad cowboy hat, way up above the ground. He glanced down at Kelly and blushed, biting his lip. On his high cheekbones, a constellation of pimples spread out in a galaxy across his skin.

'No need to go shy on me, Narra,' Kelly said, looking up at him. 'A dare is a dare. I lost it fair and square. And if you're up for it, I am too. So let's just get our gear off.'

She stooped and removed her boots, flinging them onto the dam bank, and reached for her belt buckle.

'C'mon … it'll be a hoot. Think of it as skinny dipping with extras.'

Kelly was talking bravely, but in truth, she was just as nervous. She liked Narra. *Really* liked him. And if he said no to her now, she knew she'd be cut up rough.

Narra was the latest of the new recruits on Bilga Station, and for a jackaroo, Kelly thought, he was more than 'not bad'. If you looked past the pimples and the fact he looked like a ute's aerial, Narra could be considered cute. Over the past few years on Bilga, some of the boys who had come and gone from her musterer's swag had been arseholes, but not Narra. There was something about him that made him stand out, and she knew it wasn't just his almost seven-foot height. She smiled every time she saw him and found herself hoping the overseer would team them up together again. She liked just being around him. He may not have been the handsomest, but he was the sweetest fella Kelly'd ever found on the place. He stayed clear of trouble and came out with the wittiest of one-liners at perfectly timed moments, grinning a crooked grin.

While this was Narra's first muster and cattle drive, Kelly had been at the work for three seasons now. She'd gone from jillaroo to the drovers' team leader. It had been good to climb the ranks towards her goal of overseer. Most of the girls only came for the one year, but not Kelly. She'd stuck it out and earned her stripes, wearing her nickname of Sparra proudly amongst the men.

The work was hard and the days were hot, but she liked the company of dirty, dusty men and women who soaked their troubles away with a cold beer and rum in the evenings. Social life was mostly played out on the station. It was too far to the pub in town, three hours' drive away. So, in the evenings, they would gather with a box of beer and hang on the yard railings as each of them worked stockhorses round the cattle for a bit of social competition, as was their way.

The horses were the main reason Kelly loved her job so much. There were some good types on the station, well-bred creatures from Australian stockhorse bloodlines and quarter horse stock, but for this mustering trip the very best nags had been left behind because there was a big draft near Mt Isa next week. The tidiest, most talented horses had been spelled back at the homestead, so the horse droving team this trip was a mixed bag of 'the seconds', including Kelly's back-up horse, Motley. Her boss had given Motley to Sparra because the horse was the most spindle-legged mare on Bilga and was as lightly boned as Kelly. The men were too heavy to ride her, or if they were light enough, weren't game to. The flecked, undernourished grey that had been caught as a brumby foal was a sweetie on the ground for anyone handling her, but under saddle and mounted when fresh in the early mornings, she would proceed to buck like a pro-rodeo bull. But Kelly was a tough little rider. Not once in three years had the mare tipped Kelly into the dirt. The team thought Motley and Sparra made a great pair, and thought the same of Narra and his massively wide horse, Gordon, a big droop-lipped Clydesdale cross who had been around for so long that no one remembered where the patchy horse of white and brown, with feathery hocks, had come from.

Soon Narra and Sparra were making a great team too. They had become good mates on the two-week long muster and drove, but now Kelly wanted more than 'just mates'. This was her last chance to fire something up between them. She stood with her horse beside the edge of the dam, looking at Narra, the challenge she'd thrown down to him lying between them.

'Well? Are you in?'

Narra grinned. 'Are you for real, Sparra? Are you sure?'

Kelly grinned back. 'Why not? Blame Snooza if you like, but I reckon we oughta give it a burl,' she said with a gleam in her eye. She drew her leather hobble belt from the loops of her jeans and squatted before Motley, fixing the hobble around the mare's skinny fetlocks. The grey laid her ears back and swished her tail, disgruntled she wasn't travelling back with the rest of the horses to her home paddock.

Standing, Kelly began to unbutton her jeans. When Narra saw Kelly was for real, an expression of utter terror combined with sheer excitement slid across his face. Following Kelly's cue, Narra dropped the reins of his big feather-footed Clydey. He stooped to scoop off his boots, cast off his hat, hastily drew his T-shirt over his head and dropped his strides. Kelly matched him so that within seconds they both stood starkers, grinning at each other.

'Get him naked too,' she said, nodding to Narra's horse, Gordon.

Within an instant, Narra had uncinched the girth and thrown the big stock saddle to the ground, the smell of pungent horse sweat releasing from the soaked and dusty saddlecloth. Then both Sparra and Narra began leading Gordon into the dam, the warm brown water washing up over their hot dusty legs, the mud squelching between their toes and laughter bubbling up. When Gordon was knee-deep, he began pawing the water with his big cannon-boned legs, frothing brown droplets of muddy sodic dam water all over them.

'Gordy!' squealed Kelly as she felt the blissful cool of the water splash onto her sun-parched skin, making her nipples rise.

'I can't believe we're doing this,' Narra said, glancing over at her, taking in her little pink rosebud breasts and lean white stomach … a stark contrast to her deeply tanned arms and chest. He felt his penis starting to fill, and hoped they would move deeper in the water so Kelly wouldn't see his desire.

'Well, we've got to prove Snooza wrong …' Kelly said, 'and …' she turned to face him and reached for his hand, 'I really want to.'

Narra swallowed again and squeezed her tiny hand. 'I really want to too. With you,' he said.

He looked at her with such sincerity and such a lonely boyish innocence, that right at that moment, under the bright outback sun, Kelly felt her heart melt.

The reason the pair were in the dam had started on stock camp the night before, when Snooza had driven the truck out to help pack up the droving camp. As they sat about the campfire, the dry wood crackling bright sparks into the dark night, Snooza had looked over to the crew of horses tied on the night lines between two scraggly trees and said of Gordon for the fiftieth time, 'He's so quiet, that horse, you could have a bonk on him.' Then he'd slowly swigged his rum, shaken his head, kicked the dust with the toe of his boot and said again, 'Yep. I reckon that horse is so quiet, you could have a bonk on him.'

The mustering and droving team, a bit full on rum and beer due to the fact it was their last night camped out, had made their way over to the big old draught horse to view the width and flatness of his back. A conversation ensued with the dusty and drunk crew standing about looking at Gordon and trying to figure out how two people would go about having a bonk on a horse. What would be the most effective position? Would the old horse stand still? Would he be best tied or hobbled? The conversation lingered on late into the night until the campfire was just smoke and ash and most of the team had drifted away to their swags.

It was Narra and Sparra who, lying in their swags next to each other, still talking dribbling drunken shit about Gordon, finally did a rock, paper, scissors best of three on the matter. The dare was that Kelly would give it a go bonking Narra on the horse, to see if what Snooza said was true. Under the bright twinkle of midnight stars, Kelly had lost with her scissors to Narra's rock and the secret deal was set.

Everyone was quiet on the next day's droving. Hangovers took up the morning, made a little better by lunch, but as boredom and heat exhaustion set in as they tailed the cattle for home, all Kelly could think of was the cool dam that they would reach by that afternoon and getting Narra naked on his wide-backed horse. She was glad she had lost the bet. She was feeling the sexual tension build in her body as she sat astride Motley. She couldn't wait to get to the dam and send the rest of the plant ahead, offering up the excuse that Narra and she would ride on a bit and check a windmill and a bore a few kilometres to the east on the way home.

Now, in the water, she could sense Narra's arousal building. His hunger for her. She moved closer and drew him in under the water, her tiny breasts brushing his chest. The world morphed into wetness and darkness as they reached for each other beneath the surface. Fingertips met with skin. Palms on flesh. Her torso pressed wet to his. She felt the nudge of his erection and when they surfaced, they were kissing, Narra bending his long body down and over to reach her lips. His huge hands spanned the bulk of her tiny back. The hard point of his erect cock feathered her nipples every now and then. She felt a giggle rise up in her. He was so tall, if he stood straight, Kelly thought, she could put his dick in her mouth without even bending down. She made a mental note to herself to try that with him later, but first things first: Snooza's insisting that 'that horse is so quiet you could have a bonk on him'.

'Let's get started,' Kelly said, leading Narra by the hand deeper into the dam, Narra in turn leading Gordon with them. When the horse was in up to his shoulder, Kelly said, 'Bunk me up.'

And right away Narra was lifting her up, naked, onto the hot, dusty and sweat-crusted back of Gordon. She felt the odd sensation of her bare bum on the skin of the animal and looked down to her legs that barely reached down his side. They stuck out like she was a little kid on a pony ride. It was then Kelly lost it. She began laughing and could not stop. Narra began to laugh too.

'Oh, man, this is crazy,' he said with his cute crooked grin, blue-grey eyes shining, eyes that were framed by long, wet dark eyelashes.

'How do you ride this thing! He's huge! And he's so hot he's burning my arse cheeks.' Narra lifted his head to the sky, laughing harder, and Kelly caught a flash of perfect white teeth.

'I'll take him deeper,' he said, and soon the horse and Narra were being swallowed up by the waters and Kelly could feel the coldness of the dam rising up and over the back of Gordon and meeting with her hot sex.

'Do you reckon this counts as bestiality?' she said jokingly.

Narra frowned. 'Jeez. I hadn't thought of that.'

'Maybe don't think of it! It's a bit of a turn-off.'

'You're not a turn-off,' Narra said quietly.

Kelly felt her heart thudding in her chest. He did want her.

'Well, c'mon, Casanova,' she said with forced casualness, 'up you get!' Like a circus performer, Kelly placed her hands on Gordon's neck and plonked herself forward onto his withers so Narra had room to swing up behind her. When he was on, she felt the wet press of his warm torso against the bare skin of her back and couldn't help the gasp that escaped from her. The laughter and the humour of the moment slipped away and flowed into something else. Another kind of mood. One of desire.

She felt a rush. Narra put his hands on her waist and dropped his head down towards her, kissing her along the line of her neck. She felt his cock fill and press against her small wet buttocks. Gordy shifted suddenly, wanting to go deeper and swim. The big gelding pivoted on his hindquarters and spun about.

'Whoa!' Kelly said, nearly pitching off sideways. She drew the giant horse around with one rein and steadied him. 'Snooza may be wrong.'

'I'm not giving up yet,' murmured Narra, who kept on with his kissing, his lips searching out her ear lobes, and she could feel the goosebumps sweeping over her skin, her nipples growing pebble hard. She felt a longing to have him penetrate her so she lifted herself a little and tilted her arse back towards his cock, but when she tried to lower herself onto him the water stole the juices from them so that the friction burnt.

'It isn't going to work this way,' Narra said. 'You'll have to spin around.'

Like an agile trick rider, Kelly swung a leg over the neck of the horse and was soon facing Narra, looking up into his eyes and settling her arms around his waist.

'Is that better?'

She reached up and began to kiss him, slowly, invitingly. Soon their passion was flooding them and he lifted her up onto his cock. Kelly cried out with relief as she felt him push deep inside her, her legs folding around him. With his large strong hands, he moved her up and down on his wet shaft. As Narra began to bounce Kelly on his lap, the horse took a spin again, nearly upending them into the dam.

'Hey!' Kelly cried out, flinging her arms around Narra's neck and squealing as Gordy made for the dam's bank. Narra reached around Kelly to grapple for the split reins that were cast over the gelding's neck. Kelly dissolved into hysterical laughter at the big stepping movement of the giant horse and the whooshing of water about them as he galumphed forward. The action caused Narra's cock to bounce deep inside her with every jolt of the Clydey's trot.

'This is kinda nice,' chuckled Kelly, 'but can you slow him up a bit!'

'I've lost his reins,' Narra said as his wet body slithered and slammed against hers with each lope of the horse. He grabbed hold of Kelly tighter as Gordon gained pace, making for shore. Kelly was screeching now with laughter, clinging desperately to Narra as she rode backwards.

'I think we should bail!' Narra said, but before they could fling themselves sideways into the water, Gordy made the shore and took a giant leap for the steep rise of the dam bank.

'Too late!' cried Kelly.

He gave one big lunge, his dinner-plate hooves slipping on the clay. Stepping on the rein, the bit jerked in his mouth and made Gordy pull up short. Suddenly Narra and Kelly were being catapulted sideways. They hit the greasy dam bank with a thud, slithering for a metre or so. Then came the expulsion of conjoined laughter, the sound rising up to the big blue cloudless sky. As they lay on their backs, panting hard, limbs entwined, they fell silent.

'You okay?' Narra asked eventually.

Kelly nodded. 'Who said this horse was quiet enough to bonk on! Bloody Snooza,' she said. She turned to Narra and stroked a streak of clay with her index finger across his cheek. 'At least we gave it a shot.'

'It was fun,' he said, marking her cheek with clay also.

'Oh, it's not over yet, Narra, my friend,' she said. 'Shall we forget the horse and try without?'

He propped himself up on one elbow, smiled at her and nodded.

'Wait there,' she said.

Naked and smeared with mud and clay, Kelly stood and tiptoed up the dam bank to Narra's pile of clothes, where she dragged the hobble belt from his jeans.

'I'll sort Gordy out for you, then I'll be back to sort you.'

She walked over to Gordon, who stood grazing next to Motley, water dripping off his coat, and clearing his nostrils with long vibrating snorts, settling himself. Kelly looped the belt around his feathery fetlocks. Then she stooped again at Motley's hocks and retrieved her hobble belt. It thrilled her to know that behind her, Narra was watching her body move about the place naked. She knew also that when she returned, his desire for her would be back in the form of a hard long cock. With her belt in hand, she slipped down the dam bank towards him and stood above him. She cast her eyes widely at him and the corner of her mouth turned up in a suggestive grin. The afternoon sun was behind her, shadowing her downy bush, and her legs were spread a little. Her eyes feasted over his long body that ran in perfect lines down to the springing invitation of his big cock. She dropped onto him, straddling him, and placed his hands above his head, took her belt and looped one loop round Narra's wrist, then fixed the buckle firmly on the other. As she did, her nipples lightly roamed above his face. She felt his mouth searching out her breasts to suck. She reefed the hobbled belt to the last hole.

'I'm not letting you get away, you bad, bad cleanskin bull,' she said.

Narra bit his bottom lip and grinned at her. 'Oh, Kelly,' he said.

It was the first time he had used her proper name. She felt another wave of wanting for him.

She lowered herself down, lying her tiny body over his, kissing the skin of him. He tasted of outback soil, sun and freedom. And there on the dam bank the mini-jillaroo rode her favourite long, thin jackaroo until she was bucking back and forth. It took no time for her to come in shuddering waves, her pussy clutching him tightly, moistly.

Barely satisfied with just one orgasm, she dropped forward to kiss him passionately, then, as she did on the horse, lifted herself and spun about on his hard erection. Facing the dam now, she reached forward to grasp the long muscles of his thighs as she pumped her little body up and down on him again, the angle of his penis causing monumental pleasures within her. She heard Narra groan as he lifted his head and took in the arousing sight of her pert little backside and her tight little muff swallowing up his cock before his eyes. He couldn't touch her. His wrists strained against the belt. Pinned on the dam bank by the pint-sized jillaroo galloping on him, Narra moaned. She rode him faster and felt the nub of his cock deep within her, moving her to another sexual peak. As she came again, her pussy pulsed in orgasmic waves around his cock. It was too much for him. He exploded into her, the juices of their lovemaking combining with the dam water and clay smeared over their bellies and thighs.

When she had felt the last shuddering wave of pleasure run through her body, Kelly pivoted around to face Narra and, still sitting astride him, gave him a gorgeous smile. His arms, still hobbled, were cast above his head, his knuckles white from the agonising pleasure of it all.

'You didn't buck me off,' Kelly said.

'I tried,' he said, grinning.

As she reached to unbuckle the belt from his wrists, she glanced up. Motley had gone. The mare had obviously decided to make her own way back to the homestead, leaving Gordy to himself.

'Cranky horse. She's cleared out on us. I knew she would.'

'Looks like we'll have to dink back on Gordon,' Narra said with flirtation in his voice.

'I go in front,' she said.

'Again! We could give it another shot on the way,' Narra said. 'Prove Snooza correct.' And they both laughed.

And together as they splashed into the water to wash the sex and mud from their bodies, they smiled at each other, knowing they were in for many more rides at Bilga Station and the droving was far from done.

Fifty Bales of Hay

*I*t was almost that time of the month for Carrie and she was wallowing in a cranky-pants mood she just couldn't shift. Neither the brightest of summer mornings nor the overzealous tail wagging from curly-coated Muppet could jolt her out of her pre-menstrual grump. Instead, she shut the dog in the laundry and, with a stainless-steel bowl cradled in the bend of her long brown arm, trudged in Zac's gumboots up to the top end of the raspberry paddock. There she climbed the steepest pitch of the hillside, her elegant, toned legs straining with every step. A frown on her face. Her heart heavy.

It was here on this sharp slope that Carrie knew she would find the juiciest berries clustering thickly under the sheltering leaves. This was the part of the farm where the 'Pick Your Own' tourists were too lazy to haul themselves up the last steep incline. The visitors were more likely to be found in the strawberry paddocks beside the dam, or sipping lattes under the café umbrellas at the cottage — picking raspberries and strawberries became tiresome for most, once the novelty wore off. Carrie herself had discovered early that a kind of mental meditation was needed for the lengthy, sometimes tedious, task.

High on the hills, stooping over her lush prolific canes that grew in long sweeping rows down the face of the slope, Carrie began to draw the bulbous red berries from their hiding places beneath large dank green leaves. An early morning blowie buzzed by. It was going to be a stinker, Carrie thought. The sun was barely up, but already she could feel the drowsiness of a heatwave settling over the landscape. She stood, arched her back to stretch a little, and moved along the row. As she did, she looked beyond the cottage and the Summerberry Shop to the distance where a subdued sea drew a neat blue line on the horizon. Not even the spectacular vista cast before her, the undulating bush-covered hills patched occasionally with summertime paddocks of rich farmland, nor the astoundingly pretty sweep of the white beaches of Moonlight Bay, moved any kind of joy within her.

'Just put on your big cowgirl boots and deal with it,' she told herself angrily.

Carrie had a plan to combat her chronic shittyness. She would go inside the little cottage, douse her fresh berries with bucketloads of organic cream, top them with a sprinkling of dark chocolate and wash it all down with the strongest of coffees, made from the Moonlight Bay Summerberry Shop's fancy café machine that had cost her and Zac a bomb. Then she planned on washing her hair, getting properly dressed in something very summery and pretty, and plastering a smile on her face after she'd set the 'Open' sign out on the road. She wanted the people to come.

She had to be charming. Maybe they would buy some of her artwork. God knows she needed their money!

As she picked her breakfast berries, she wondered if she'd have enough time to dig her old vibrator out of the bedside drawer, pilfer a few batteries from the TV remote and give herself some orgasm therapy. Maybe *that* would help her transcend her mood. But then Carrie groaned internally, because she knew the vibrator wouldn't cut it and she'd cry afterwards. No, not just cry. She'd sob, lying there with a piece of no-longer-buzzing plastic in her hand, post-lonely orgasm, wondering why life should be so cruel to a woman. And not just any woman, but a woman as good and as attractive as she was. A woman who was kind. And giving.

Perhaps a little overwrought and pedantic at times … but a goddess nonetheless … on the right days. She could be a touch on the stormy side, she conceded. Like the time she'd been so mad at Zac she had filled one of his Ugg boots with water and chucked it onto the lawn one frosty night.

Her mouth twisted tensely from side to side as she thought of the vibrator again. Best not to go there. It would only underscore her loneliness. It would be like putting a burning match near something flammable.

She'd never really liked Mr Pink, as Zac had called it, anyway. He'd brought the thing home and had thrust the giftwrapped box at her, saying, 'Now you won't miss me when I'm away. You've got this to do the job. Might ease your tension.' She'd taken the package and his subtle dig with a giggle at first, but then she had frowned.

'Where'd you buy it?'

Zac had looked down to the toes of his regulation mining company steel-cap boots. 'Sex shop,' he'd mumbled.

'Where? What were you doing in a sex shop?' Her voice taking on *that* tone.

'Perth. You know. The boys.'

Carrie had harrumphed and thrust the box back at him.

'Jeez, Carrie,' Zac had said, 'they're like supermarkets now. I was shopping for you. Me and the fellas. I thought you'd like something to tickle your fancy.'

'My fancy?'

And the whole moment had deteriorated from there.

Since that time, Mr Pink had always carried with him the tainted reminder for Carrie that: a) she never really knew what Zac was up to, and b) her quiet inner knowledge that they weren't suited to each other. He just didn't 'get' her.

Her rumbling of mistrust and their growing differences seemed to feed every kind of trouble between them. Plus, bloody Zac was always blaming her moods on the fact she was 'a creative type', or on her menstrual cycle, which was vastly unfair, Carrie had argued. Sure she was artistic, but she could be cranky any time.

Maybe today's lethargy and depression were to do with the fluctuations of her hormones, but that was only a thin veil covering a volcanic anger that had everything to do with Zac's leaving. She rubber-rafted her lips with breath, the vibration making a noise like a snorting horse, and tucked a strand of long blonde hair escaping from what was yesterday's ponytail behind her delicate ear. She was sick of thinking about it over and over. But she couldn't help herself.

She couldn't figure what had turned Zac from being her live-in boyfriend of five years into a receding memory. One moment she had a gorgeous mining man who worked two weeks on and two weeks off, bringing home good bacon; the next she had a man who had worked his two weeks on and then *completely* pissed off. Carrie felt another wave of fury that he'd done a runner.

There was still so much to do on the farm and the income was sporadic and horribly seasonal to say the least. He'd been gone three months now. There was no time for her painting. There was no money for staff, so she had to do everything herself: harvesting, marketing, branding, coffee grinding, ice-cream making … *the works*. It was exhausting. To top it all off, there'd been not a word from him. Only rumours on the wind, from his mates, that ('maybe') he'd met some smoking-hot Asian-Aussie woman on his transit through Broome and had fallen passionately in lust.

'Fuck it all,' Carrie said as she picked more berries than needed for breakfast. She resolved to use the excess berries tonight after work. She would make herself a stiff raspberry crush vodka or three, get plastered by herself and wonder why a woman as gorgeous as herself was left alone on a very pretty, but very lonely, farm with just a tethered goat, a shitzoodle type of fluffy black dog and five near-wool blind sheep. And acres and acres of goddamned berries!

Down below in the house, she could hear the faint yips of Muppet coming from the laundry. She looked up and heard the rumble of a vehicle approaching along the highway, then a gear change down as the driver turned into the dirt road to her place.

'Fuck it,' she said again as she saw flashes of a small white truck through the canopy of the trees that lined the road. She looked down at what she was wearing. Barely anything. Just her little ripped denim mini that hardly covered her arse and the skimpy floral singlet she'd thrown on over her swollen, aching pre-menstrual breasts.

'Fuck, fuck, fuck it!' She hated visitors arriving before ten in the morning. Especially when she had the shits like this.

'Double double treble fuck it,' she said when she saw the truck was from Robertson's Rural Supplies and was teetering with a load of oddments for the other farms in the district and her order of straw for the raspberries. It wasn't the time of year to mulch, but the summer had been dry and the dams were looking low, so Carrie thought she ought to do something to help preserve the moisture on the area of the farm where the soil was thinner and less fertile, just above the cottage. A second layer of straw couldn't hurt. She already had a few bales she'd bought from a roadside stall last week sitting ready to spread on the strawberries too. When she got a moment.

She looked again to what she was wearing. Buggered if she wanted to help old Fred from the rural supply company unload bales in this get-up. She'd basically just rolled out of bed and hadn't bothered to put on a bra or knickers.

Old Fred would probably crack a fat when he saw her, the blood rushing from his heart to his dick, and he'd have a coronary on the spot. Then she'd have to call an ambulance, give him CPR, which would not be a pleasant thing, all the while having to deal with how inconvenient it was, as she hadn't yet had a shower, let alone had time to have her fucking breakfast.

Angrily she began to stomp down the hill, wondering why the Robertson's Rural Supplies bastards couldn't have had the courtesy to phone before they left the store. How did they know she would be up at this hour of the morning? Didn't they realise she could still be in bed with some fabulous spunky lover, and not wanting to unload straw at the crack of dawn? Instead, wanting to go down on her lover's morning crack of fat. She sighed as Zac's big rubber boots made sloppy slapping sounds against her tanned bare legs while the pitch of the hill began to give her momentum. She gathered speed. Too much speed. She held the bowl on one hip as she angled her feet and body sideways to slow herself. She imagined herself running uncontrollably down the hill and landing, splat, berries and all, at the feet of Fred with her bare arse in the air for the world to see. That would finish off the pervy old bugger.

She had to watch her footing, so it wasn't until she was on more even ground that Carrie looked again at the truck.

She saw the man, who certainly wasn't Fred, get out in the berry farm parking area and stand with his hands on his narrow hips, his back to her, looking down the slope of the hill to the valley below and the view of Moonlight Bay. It would be so nice to go to the beach today, she thought, and no doubt the man was thinking the same. She took in his extremely nice legs running up to denim shorts cupping a very tidy backside that tapered into a thin waist, then out again to perfect Brad Pitt broad shoulders. He began to walk over to the house, where Muppet was going off her tits in the laundry. Behind him Carrie yelled out, 'Helloooo!' as she stood in the raspberry patch halfway down the hill.

The bloke spun around and stood with one hand on his hip, the other held above his brow against the morning glare, looked up the hill and gave her a 'G'day!' back. He waved and then started untying the ropes on the truck. Muttering, Carrie made her way down to him, wondering where Fred was and how on earth she would get past this new Robertson bloke and into the house without him seeing her beaver since it was practically hanging out below her short, short skirt. She had sadly neglected it since Zac had been gone. It was like a summer raspberry patch itself, left to grow wild. Those Robertson blokes were rude bastards not calling. She tugged down her skirt. The volcano bubbled and stirred …

'Good morning!' the bloke said cheerfully, dropping the ropes and walking over to her, his hand extended. 'Joey,' he said.

She was trying hard to block out the fact he was one of the most delicious men she had ever seen. He had 'naughty, but nice' eyes the same colour as the summertime sea behind him, a classically surfer-boy-cheeky angular face and blond curling locks that moved when he turned his head and sat tantalisingly long against his smooth neck.

She extended her hand and he clasped her raspberry-pink stained fingertips and looked dreamily into her eyes. For a nanosecond. Then she saw his eyes slide downwards, and without any form of self-consciousness he blatantly drank in the sight of her near to naked body. His eyes slid back up to hers and he tilted his head a little cockily to the side and grinned at her with appreciation.

'Now it really *is* a good morning,' he said flirtily. 'I hope every farmer on this delivery run turns out to look like you!'

She blew a dragon's breath from her nostrils and rolled her eyes. Boring, she almost said out loud. Since her teenage years, she knew the drill with men. It was so predictable. Her appearance fitted the ideal formula for most of them: long blonde hair, long tanned limbs, biggish norks, slim waist, grabbable arse and big blue eyes. Carrie barely stopped herself from shaking her head. She got it all the time. The wolf whistles. The catcalls. The nudge nudge, wink winks. Didn't men bloody well realise that, internally, she was more beautiful? Couldn't they see? No, they just wanted the poster version of her, like Zac had. He didn't want what was on the inside. He wanted a girl from a *People* magazine. Not a real and rounded woman. A woman with a talent for art, and passion, and willpower. Not a woman with moods and menstrual blood. And this guy was no different. Maybe, she thought, when the Summerberry Farm was closed on Monday, she could go into town and get her hair cut off. That would fix the bastards. Joey's smile quickly disappeared once Carrie spoke.

'You're frigging early,' she snapped. 'Could you *be* any earlier?'

Joey shrugged. 'Not a morning person, are we?' he said, going back to the truck and tackling the ropes again.

'Fred never came before ten,' Carrie said curtly.

'Fred never had to chase waves down at the Neck. It's rolling in. Positively pumping!'

Ah, Carrie thought, he was a surfer. And a cocky shithead one at that, with more attitude loaded in him than was loaded in the tray of his stupidly overstuffed Robertson's truck. But she noted with admiration his deliciously smooth tanned skin, as if it had been carefully polished by the sand and sea itself. And those curls! They reminded her of the exquisite spiralling patterns that could be found inside seashells. He was completely dreamy-looking.

'Well, I won't keep you from your morning,' he said with a hint of amusement at her grumpy mood. 'Where do you want your fifty bales of hay?'

'Fifty bales of hay?' Carrie asked.

'Yes,' he said, looking at his clipboard. 'Fifty bales of hay.' She made a low, angry, frustrated noise, like the rumble of a bull trying to draw a fight with his paddock mate.

'You're new, aren't you?' she said, her eyes narrowing accusingly.

'Yes. It's my first week.'

'New and incompetent,' Carrie said angrily, the volcano delivering up its first dollop of lava into the serene, still air.

She folded her arms across her breasts. 'I ordered fifty bales of *straw*. Not fifty bales of *hay*! There's a big difference, you know? Or don't you? Have you come straight from the fries counter at the local fast-food joint and this is your first proper job?'

'Look, Ms ...' Joey surveyed his delivery sheet, 'Ms *Bone*, I might be new at this job, but I didn't come down in the last shower. I know the difference between hay and straw. Same as I know the difference between manners and rudeness. Fred and Nathaniel packed the truck yesterday. I just picked it up this morning. Not my mistake, but I am sorry for it. Very sorry.'

'Passing the buck, are we? This is not good enough. I've been pouring my money into that business for years. I expect better customer service ...'

Joey flashed her a smile. A cheeky, soothing, sexy smile.

'Chill, dude! What's eating you, man? It's a beautiful day!' he said in a surfer tone that only made Carrie flush with more fury.

'What's eating me? *What's eating me? Dude?*' Carrie set the bowl down at her feet, feeling as if smoke was actually coming out of her ears and she could make entire beehives drowsy with it.

'It's only hay instead of straw. Same diff.' Joey shrugged his broad shoulders. Shoulders that Carrie couldn't help but notice looked divinely toned and strong beneath the thin cotton of his Robertson's blue work shirt. She shook the thought from her mind. For the moment, Carrie only wanted to see red. She'd had enough of men treating her as if she was a dumb, pretty little blonde. She had an entire farm and café business to run. On her own ... because her boyfriend had buggered off with some kind of Yoko Ono woman!

'Same diff? It is *not*. I wanted straw! Not hay! Straw! I can't mulch with hay — it will bring weeds to my patch.'

He grinned at her. 'Well, we can't have weeds in your patch, Ms Bone. It's cool. We can rectify things. Jeez, dude. Keep your knickers on.'

She flushed red. 'Really. My knickers. And what do you suggest I do today when this fucking sun frazzles my bushes. You are the rudest rep I've ever had. I'm going to report you.'

'Report me! For what?' He shrugged and began retying the load of hay. 'Gee, I could lose my job. Great, then I can go back to surfing. I'm sorry about your weedy patch and your frazzled bush.' He started to snigger, dipping his head up and down like a seabird as he laughed at his wit and innuendo.

'Is this your version of customer care? It's a disgrace,' she said, putting her hands on her hips. She saw Joey's eyes roam over her body again, her long summer-tanned legs, and perky breasts that could be seen through the gauzy fabric of her skimpy singlet.

'Look, lady, I don't know what's up with you today, but take a look around. It's a corker of a day. There is nothing we can't fix. Calm down. I can bring you straw this arvo. I'll even help you spread it. I'm coming back this way for my surf.'

'No! No! No!' Carrie's voice rose in tone like a squealing three-year-old about to fly into a tantrum. She bounced on the spot and briefly clenched her eyes and fists shut in frustration.

'Jeez! You on your rags or something? Look, lady, I'm only trying to help.'

A wave of indignation at what the man had said swamped Carrie. Temper fired in her like a Mack truck engine. The hurt from Zac's leaving rose up inside her when she heard the same masculine reasoning for her mood that Zac had constantly thrown at her. Fury swamped her.

'As a matter of fact, I just might be on my rags and you picked the wrong day, buddy! And you picked the wrong woman.' She grabbed for her raspberry bowl, twisted the end of Joey's sleeve into her fist, and tugged it hard so he had no choice but to follow her towards the small pile of straw bales that she'd loaded by herself from the roadside stall last week. They were nestled between the rows of raspberry canes that were clearly suffering from the extremely hot summer and the reduced waterings.

'This,' she said, angrily pointing, 'is *straw*. *That*,' she said, casting an arm to the truck, 'is hay! Look.' She set the raspberries down and began to reef at the bale twine, busting it open. Yellow stems and a sweet smell erupted into the morning air. She grabbed a fistful of the stuff and waved it in his face. 'See! See! Straw! Stalky! No seed heads. Same colour as my fucking hair!' Then she stooped and began to cast thick slabs of golden straw over the ground.

'This is straw. Totally different to hay. Get it? I didn't order fifty fucking bales of hay! I ordered straw!'

Joey reached out and grabbed her arm. 'Stop,' he said.

'Why should I?' she said, her voice breaking.

'Because you're upset and ...' he paused, '... and also because every time you bend down I can see you aren't wearing any undies.' She looked at him, shocked, and he looked back at her with a friendly, sympathetic twinkle in his eyes. He did not let go of her.

'It's all good, sister. Just chill.'

Her brow furrowed. Tears came. 'I'm ... I'm ...' she stammered, the emotions rising, unstoppable, like a southerly swell. Joey pulled her towards him and hugged her. She felt his hands travel up and down her back, soothingly.

'Shush,' he said, 'trust me. I'm good at this. I have five sisters. I can see you are mega-stressed. And I was being a bit of a git. Believe me, I know how to tease girls.'

'No ... I ... I was being angry. Not at you ... at ...'

'Hey, chill, girl,' he said. 'I can see you need help about the place. You just say how you'd like to be helped and I can help. Weeding, digging? Harvesting? I can come up after work, after my surf.'

Carrie drew back from him so she was looking into his blue-sea eyes. She didn't say a word, but Joey read the look on her face. Suddenly he knew exactly how she wanted help. And she wanted it now.

Slowly he began to run his brown hands over her bare shoulders more firmly. His touch transitioned from one of comfort to a touch of desire. She felt goosebumps rise, and the relief from his touch broke in a rhythmic wash throughout her body with his every slow, solid caress.

'Shush, you,' he said quietly to her. 'Whatever it is, it isn't that bad.'

She looked up at him, tears pooling in her eyes, and then she reached up to suddenly kiss him, drinking in the warm moisture of his generous mouth.

Next moment she was inviting him down onto the bed of straw, soaking up the blissful feeling of the weight of his masculine body on hers, the prickle of the stalks deliciously scratching her shoulder blades. His hands roamed under her singlet to her breasts, then slowly down between her legs. He murmured something deeply when his hands met with her wetness and she felt his desire build even more.

She shut her eyes and sighed with pleasure as he moved his body downwards, his face pressing against her inner thighs as he kissed and tenderly bit her skin there, his hands gently compelling her to spread her legs. Her miniskirt rose up and she watched as he grabbed a fistful of raspberries from the bowl. Next he began to smear them on her skin, starting with her inner thigh, working his way along until the wet flesh of the berries met with her sex. The pressure of his fingers and hands and the warmth of the fruit caused her to moan.

His long slender fingers moistened by berry juices began working in and out of her. Then, as she lay back, melting into the moment in a dreamy wash of pleasure, he began to eat, his lips sucking at her and the berries. Bright red juices smeared around his mouth, and in the gentle place of her vagina, the sensational melding of secretions from flesh and fruit. She felt his tongue probe inside her, then up and over her clitoris. He slid another finger deep inside her and with his mouth and hands, he pulsed movements up and down.

Carrie threw her head back, her eyes seeing electric blue as she took in the divinity of the moment and the feeling of what this man was doing to her. A butterfly drifted into her line of vision, then away on the soft breeze. Beneath her bed of straw she could sense the fecundity of the earth, the scent of the summer raspberry patch drifting over her bare skin.

As she came in a wash of sexual release and rapture, she cried out to the solo white cloud drifting above. Then Joey was on top of her and gently coaxing off her singlet top. The sight of her naked rounded breasts prompted a gasp of wanting from him and a renewed vigour of desire. He began coating her nipples with raspberry red, kissing the stain of the berries onto her body and then delivering the taste deep into her mouth. He tore off his shirt, slid down his shorts, his breath coming fast. Grabbing another fistful, Joey smeared raspberries across her breasts, then lay his bare torso on hers, the moist berries sliding across skin. Then he placed his cock deep inside her and began to slowly drive his way into her tight warmth and wetness. He reached beneath her, cupped her backside and pushed himself deeper into her. The feeling was exquisite for her. Carrie found herself lost in a lush green forest of raspberry canes and ripe berries, her mind barely registering she was being taken by a sea god.

He kneaded her flesh with fingertips and ground into her until a stellar orgasm unfolded and flowed throughout her body and took her somewhere away, up into the electric blue of summer. Her pussy clenched tightly and he felt her give way to the pleasures he had provided, just as the clamping around his cock caused him to thrust one last thrust, so he creamed into her with a moan.

They lay still for a time in the dappling of shade from the canes, looking into each other's eyes with amusement at what had just occurred. They began smearing patterns on each other's bodies with their fingers, using the berries like red henna or paint. Joey drew love hearts on her belly. She drew the word 'hay' on his. Crossed it out, then wrote 'straw'. They giggled together and tried to wipe away each other's clown-red mouths. Eventually they sat up on their soft bed of straw and he held her hand.

'You'll need a shower,' Carrie said, looking at his torso and then his Robertson's work shirt bloodied with the juice of the fruit. 'That stuff will stain like blood. You'd better come inside for a bit.'

Joey grinned at her. 'Sure. I'd love a shower. Then can I have some more raspberry tart, please?'

'Hey!' pouted Carrie. 'Are you implying I'm a tart?'

'No,' he said, cheekiness written over his face, 'I think you are berry, berry nice.' Then he kissed her deeply until Carrie got the giggles. 'Berry nice!'

And for the first time in months Carrie Bone laughed upwards from her belly and could not stop.

Cattle Crush

*T*here were now only fifty maiden heifers left to weigh, drench and fat-score in the lead-up to joining on Carnegie Downs. These girls were the last of the stragglers out of the scrub. The small herd had come in tonguing with hot breath from the run of the chopper muster, big Brahman crosses with ears drooping downwards like bloodhounds. The folds of their soft caramel-coloured hides swayed as they trotted towards their thousand compliant mates, who were already yarded up next to the bulls.

Bronwyn Hayden, better known as 'Beanbag' to her mates, hadn't been long at the ringer's job, but she was enjoying the clang and clatter of the young heifers moving through the yards. And the thrill of the muster in 4-wheelers and on horses beneath the chopper today was still zinging through her tired body. Bronwyn closed the gate of the forcing yard on the last heifer as she counted it through, and the fiftieth heifer joined the rest of the stragglers milling about. Further confined, the animals in the bugle yard that led to the draft area and the cattle crush dropped their heads, looking for an escape, and bunted each other with frustration.

'Fifty!' she called out to her workmate, Tommy.

'How many?' Tommy yelled back. He was standing near the weigh-scales, busily prepping the drench gun and rebooting the computer at the work station beside the race. The rest of the team had gone home to wash down the horses, leaving Tommy and Bronwyn to mop up the last few head of cattle.

'Fifty!' she yelled again over the mooing of the heifers, a sound this morning that came as constantly as the droning of bees, but now, thankfully, the herd had settled somewhat and patches of silence sometimes ensued about the working yards. Tommy stooped over the computer and found the data program and the file for the herd.

'You sure it wasn't sixty-nine?' he said, his fingers hovering over the keyboard, his head cocked to one side, eyes on Bronwyn.

'No, fifty!' she yelled from the back of the crush.

'What you say? Sixty-nine?' Tommy asked again.

'No! Frig you, Tommy. Not *sixty-nine*. I bloody said *fifty*!'

'Cwoor,' Tommy said, doing a swivelling happy dance with a twist of his hips. 'My favourite number!' He grinned at her from beneath his sweat-stained hat. 'I actually heard you the first time, but I wanted to hear you say sixty-nine out loud. Coz I like picturing you sittin' on me face.'

'Oh, grow up! Der!' Bronwyn rolled her eyes and laughed at how gullible she'd just been. Tommy was like that. Always catching her out on a joke, making her laugh. She shook her head and held her wry smile.

'Carn, Beanbag, we're a perfect match. Your face, my dick?'

'In your dreams, Tommy, ya dirty bugger,' Bronwyn said, pretending to be cranky. She poked her tongue out at him.

'Oi! Bring that tongue over here, Beanbag, and I'll find a use for it,' Tommy flirted.

'I bet you would too, ya feral.' She picked up a piece of poly pipe and whacked the railing hard. 'Bring your bum over here, Mr Head Stockman, and I'll give you what-for.'

'Oh, you just said head! Is that a promise?'

As she went to move the toey heifers into the forcing yard, a smile crinkled Bronwyn's eyes. Tommy was good fun to work with and she enjoyed his teasing.

When she'd first left school a couple of years back, she'd done a short stint in the city, temping, where she'd lasted two months in a government office. From that job, she knew about 'inappropriate behaviour in the workplace' because posters about it had been plastered over the walls and she'd had to do a course and fill out a question sheet. She giggled now when she thought of the place and the dorky people in it. Yep, she sighed, things were nicely different out here, in the outback, thank god. Both she and Tommy would have been done for sexual harassment fifty times over by now, if they were in that office in the big smoke. They'd practically be in gaol.

Bronwyn slipped her large frame through a side gate and slid open the back gate of the cattle crush. A scattering of galahs took flight from a battle-scarred bottle tree. The tree offered thin shade in the giant holding yard, yet most of the thousand-head herd were still trying to cluster under it.

The heifers mustered earlier that morning had settled and were now bored and hungry. A couple of the maidens who were cycling were curiously hanging around the fence near to where, beyond, the bulls waited. Some of the bull fellas sat chewing cud, one front foot cast out, the other hooves tucked under their beefy bodies, their giant balls drooping in the dust, eyes half closed in the sun. Their skin twitched and tails snapped the air at bothersome flies. The younger bulls stood bellowing to the girls at the fence and thrusting their heads low, tussling each other with long drawn-out head butts and throwing up dust with their pawing front hooves.

Bronwyn laughed at the young guns. She noticed the older bulls with the blue ear tags knew what the go was. They were the ones who were waiting patiently for the cows to be moved to their fresh paddock. The old boys knew, when the gate swung open, they would be free to amble their way to a six-week bonkfest frenzy. In the yard to Bronwyn's right were the other cows. The poor girls there were too skinny to bother with. In a drought year there was nothing to fatten them on, so it was off to the abattoir for them. No doubt Tommy would insist Bronwyn come with him in the double-decker on the trip to Rocky. She smiled at what the trip would be. A laugh and a half for sure. And maybe more?

Bronwyn looked up to the dusty sky where the setting sun hung in a big yellow ball. It was hard to believe she was here on Carnegie. The massive, beautiful stretch of a station was a far cry from the backyard where she had grown up in Drouin and her first job pulling tits for a dirty old perv of a dairy farmer on the outskirts of town. She jutted out her chin and puffed away a cluster of flies from her face with a sudden upward breath.

'Ready to roll, Tom?' she asked.

'Go for it,' he said, as she went to let the first heifer up. Yes, she thought, satisfied, she was glad she had gone outback. She stepped away a little from the railing and the first heifer ambled up. Bronwyn waited for the exact moment to pull the lever and catch the heifer's head in the crush. The vertical bars came down either side of the heifer's neck. The beast tried to push forward, then pull back. Realising she was trapped, the caramel-coloured heifer scrabbled her hooves a little against the rough, stone-rubble concrete, but then settled. Tommy arrived at the head bale with the drench gun and stooped at the head of the beast.

'Better late than never, darlin',' he said to the heifer as he stretched to press his thick fingers onto her rump. The heifer bucked a little.

'She's a keeper. I'd score her a three,' he said, then hooked the metal nozzle into the animal's mouth and gave her a shot of drench. Bronwyn typed the heifer's tag number into the computer and recorded the weight showing in the digital box on the scales.

'Congratulations, you have just scored a date with Mr Bully Boy,' Bronwyn said, watching as Tommy drafted the cow into the yard on the left.

'Not like you,' Tommy said, eyeing the next beast that Bronwyn had just pinned in the crush. 'You don't get a date. Sorry, darlin'. You score a two. Too skinny to make you a breeder.'

It was hard to see cattle in this condition, but it had been hellishly dry and now there was only room for the good doers of the herd, the ones that could hold their weight in tough times. Bronwyn noted the beast's tag number in the system as a cull before she let her go. She was getting the hang of working the Queensland beef cattle. More so still, she was getting the hang of Tommy Reynolds. He had been a total flirt with her from the start. Been at her for three months since she'd first arrived, saying she had, 'real pretty eyes. Like a collie-dog bitch.' He'd started this morning at the yards, slapping her on her broad arse and winking as he said, 'I'd like to fat-score you, Beanbag baby.'

She'd grinned back at him. 'Too much there for you to handle, mate. Most men don't even bother to try. They go for the skinny ones. Not ones like me.'

'I ain't most men.' He'd pointed at the heifers. 'We're fat-scorin' these, coz the skinny ones are out the gate to the meat works … it's the fatter ones we want for joining with the bulls. Better to get a calf out of them ones. And I'm after the same for meself. I like the fuller types,' he'd said with another wink as he ambled away, whacking a piece of poly pipe against his thigh. Loudly he began to sing a somewhat toneless version of Queen's 'Fat Bottomed Girls' then let out a hollering whoop up to the big wide sky. She watched as his chunky form receded into the dust of the cattle in the yard so all she could see was his R.M. Williams, Big Men's size, blue work shirt.

Bronwyn had always liked big fellas. Tommy looked good in Dogger boots and she liked the way his sideburns emerged from beneath his hat, like a cowboy version of Elvis after he'd eaten all those burgers and fries. As she'd watched Tommy dodge a toey beast and leap for the rail, she suddenly realised she'd like to know what tools he had hiding beneath that big verandah of his. She'd been through a bit of a dry spell with men. Some were none too keen on her size, but not Tommy. He'd been trying to get into her pants for weeks with his constant flirting. She'd been holding off for Tank, the grader driver, but he'd been gone now for over a month. And, she had realised, he wasn't as much fun as Tommy.

As the hot dusty days rolled by, Bronwyn had begun to look forward to Tommy's company and his stirring. Like last Saturday's bore run when he'd flicked water at her from the trough, shouting, 'Wet T-shirt! Wet T-shirt!' Or how he sat far too close to her in the truck on the way to the top yards on Tuesday. She liked the way he smelled of rollie tobacco, Lynx deodorant and proper man's sweat. The other night, round the Laminex table in the crib room, Bronwyn had thought for a moment he would kiss her, but instead, even though he was well lubricated on Bundy Red, he'd shyly said, 'Goodnight, beautiful bouncy Beanbag,' and stooped to kiss her hand. Then he'd walked away, wobbling a little in his boots, disturbing the cane toads that sat like stones on the buffalo grass.

Now, as she eyed Tommy's strong hands and sexy tanned forearms, Bronwyn resolved it was time to open the gate for Tommy. In the same way she would open the gate at the bulls paddock this evening. Subtly she turned away from him, made sure he wasn't looking, then undid one extra button on her work shirt. She shuffled her big tits upwards a little more in her bra, tugged her shirt even lower, then got about working the cows through the yard. She had a plan. She wanted Tommy. And she would have him.

The last of the cattle flowed through the yard easy-peasy, their weights recorded on the computer, the drench pack just lasting the distance until the final heifer pulled back from the release of the crush. The heifer saw her chance at the opened head bale and tumbled forward, jogging over to her mates.

'Job well done, Beanbag girl,' Tommy said, clapping her on the shoulder. She felt his big thick fingers press into the flesh of her upper arm. She saw his eyes brush over her deep, tanned cleavage. She felt a buzz. She knew she had him, if she wanted him. She chewed her lip for a second.

'You missed one,' she said.

Tommy's eyes scanned the forcing yard, his head tilted to the side, puzzled. There were no cattle left there.

'What about me? You didn't fat-score me,' she said, jutting out her hip, turning her backside to him and slapping her own rump hard with the flat of her hand.

'Oh, I'll score you alright,' Tommy said, grinning at her.

'I'm serious,' she said. 'I've got a serious crush on you.'

'You have?'

She nodded, jerking open the side gate of the cattle crush and stepping in. She stood waiting at the head bale, eyeing him with her big brown collie-dog eyes, hungry for a feed. She bent forward.

'Go on. Dare you,' she said, wiggling her ample rump at him, running her hands on her thick and meaty thighs. 'Pin me in.'

Tommy swallowed, his eyes darting from the head bale lever to her. He hesitated.

'Quick, or I'll get away,' Bronwyn said. She turned to him, her voice low, like the bulls droning to be let in with the cows. 'I want you, Tommy. I want you bad. From behind.'

'Oh, jeez, woman,' Tommy breathed. 'You sure?'

She nodded and smiled.

Tommy sucked in a breath. 'I want you too,' he said huskily.

Tommy reached for the lever. He pulled gently down so the metal ratchet clanked and the bale closed in around Bronwyn's shoulders. With her head caught in the cattle crush, Bronwyn felt her pulse quicken and her horniness glimmer across her skin, making her giant nipples rise to two hard lumps. She felt a desperation, she felt she wanted to be filled up by Tommy, to be slammed by him, to be utterly taken. How long had it been?

Hastily, with her breath coming fast, she began to undo her belt buckle. She heard Tommy step into the crush behind her. She heard his rodeo buckle clank a little as he undid it. Then when she felt his touch on the skin of her back, wetness soaked into her panties. Giving him a helping hand, they both began to tug her dusty jeans over the curves of her buttocks. Stripped bare from the waist down, with her arse pointed roundly to the man who stood before it, Bronwyn thought she would scream out in frustration if he didn't plunge into her there and then.

'Oh, god, that's beautiful,' she heard him murmur. Suddenly she felt the rough skin of his hands roving gently up and over her giant rump and heard his quavering sigh, as if this delivery into his life was something like an answered prayer. She felt his hot sweating cheek pressed against the white dome of one of her arse cheeks, his sideburns prickling just a little.

'Oh, god, that's beautiful,' he said again, his fingers palpitating her dimpled flesh. His touch got firmer. Her desire ran thickly in her. Then he bit her. Her cry was sudden. The pain speared through her, delightfully. His mouth warm and wet, his teeth sharp, but the bite gentle enough so the pain and pleasure blended into bliss. She jolted.

'Again,' she said, 'bite me again.' It felt painfully addictive. He sunk his teeth into her dimpled flesh and began to suck. This time harder. Her skin bruised. Mottled where his mouth had been. Bronwyn screamed out. Her cry seemed to open the gate in him. She heard his quickened breath. His frantic hands grabbing, kneading, moulding her flesh, his fingers searching out her cunt until he began dipping deeply in and out of her wetness. Thumb inside her, his other fingers pressing hard and fast on her clitoris. She bucked against him, her boots scrabbling on the concrete of the race.

'Fuck me, please, Tom. Now.' Then she felt his short thick cock plunge inside her. His hands gripped her hips and he slammed into her. She felt the delicious weight of his stomach hitting against her backside. Gritting her teeth against his thrusts, Bronwyn had to grab the sides of the cattle rails to steady herself. Her shoulders collected on the crush, and the solidity of the metal against her body felt good. Next his hands grappling for her tits. She heard his cry of pleasure as his hands roamed over the enormity of them.

'Oh, god,' he said, his mind drifting up somewhere to the ether of the outback sky. He pressured himself against her deeply and ground into her. Suddenly the stub of his cock hit a pleasure zone she didn't know she had. An orgasm exploded and rushed through her body, causing a deep throaty bellow from her opened mouth. As she felt Tommy let go inside her and heard him cry out, she smiled, feeling the thick pulse of his cock.

Tommy stood for a time panting hard, stroking her backside gently as if it was the sides of a sheened and special horse. He stooped to kiss her on each large moonscape of her rounded bottom, then he helped draw her knickers and jeans up from where they were draped above her dusty work boots. He dragged up his own trousers and stepped out of the crush, pulled on the lever and released Bronwyn from the bale.

They rearranged their clothing in silence, breathing heavily, reeling from the surreal encounter, feeling the earth settle back under their boots. Then, in the glowing light of the outback sun, Tommy passed Bronwyn his water cooler and jammed her hat back on her head.

'You just made my day, Beanbag,' Tommy said. 'In fact, you just made my life.'

'But,' she said with a cheekiness in her tone, 'you haven't finished your job? What's your score?'

Tommy pushed his thick fingers up under his hat and scratched his sweat-soaked black hair. He shook his head and his mouth opened up into a wide smile.

'Off the scales, mate. But if you need a number, I'd score you a ten. Definitely a ten out of ten. You're a keeper for sure.'

Truck Wash

*C*elia knew there was a good truck wash ahead, at a big set of saleyards about fifty kilometres out of Brisbane. She remembered pointing out the saleyards to Brian about six years ago. She had then made a suggestive comment about what she wanted to do with him when they got there. He had grabbed her hand as he drove the 18-wheeler and pressed her palm over the erection that was bulging inside his KingGee shorts. As Celia moved to change lanes, she glanced into the big oblong rear-view mirror of the truck to check for traffic and tensed her jaw. Those days with Brian as part of the driving partnership were long gone.

She sighed as she held onto the wheel, twisted her back a little and stretched. Then she flexed the muscles of her clutch leg, noticing her accelerator leg had caught too much sun through the window and was red compared to the tan of her other leg. She'd be so glad to get to the truck wash and have a bit of a walk and a cooldown in that splashing water. Celia knew it would be good to give the old girl a squirt before she pulled into the overnight motel on the outskirts of Brizzie, so the truck was clean when she picked up her backload of cattle tomorrow morning. And she didn't want to pong out the motel either, parked there overnight. Anyway, it was always a good idea to tackle the manure and urine while it was fresh; blast it out so it didn't corrode the steel any more than it already did. It gave the trucks a longer lease of life too. God knows the trucks cost them a fortune. If only Brian would agree, she'd sell the lot of them and retire early. She often pictured herself lying in a tiny bikini on the verandah of one of those marina-style houses in Queensland. Maybe she should forget the backload of cattle, forget Brian and shift up here. She liked the sunshine.

At the 'Livestock Selling Centre' sign Celia dropped back a gear, felt the Mack truck ease off, rattling the ramps in the empty stock crate a little as the engine changed its thrum. She wondered if she should call Brian to say she'd delivered the sheep okay. But then, she thought bitterly, what would he care? She was sure he'd sent her on this long haul from Victoria just to get her out of the house and out of what was left of his hair. They had been arguing a lot lately, and in the aftermath of their fights they stalked around each other like cantankerous cats who had brawled enough to pull fur, but not enough to draw blood.

For the past two days of driving, Celia had drifted from anger, hurt and bitterness over Brian, to a loneliness, a longing and a horniness beyond belief. On the rougher roads, the vibrations of the truck had shimmered through the seams of her denim shorts, turning her on at the same time as rattling a dull misery into her that had settled in the pit of her stomach like a slow-moving stomach-ache. Celia longed for something exciting to happen in her life.

Anything. Anything to move her forward from the mire her life had become.

The closest she got to fun these days was cranking her *Best of Alan Jackson* CD to full throttle in the truck and winding down the window to let a blast of hot air ruffle up her bleached-blonde curly hair. Sometimes, for a laugh, she'd let out her ponytail and pull her singlet top down real, real low for the interstate drivers to gawp at on a slow cat-and-mouse double-lane pass. Even though she had no cleavage to speak of, she sometimes got the solid blast of an air horn in appreciation from one of the other truckers. But other than that (and maybe a Bundy at the end of the day), that was it. Her list of fun in life. Full stop.

All she had these days were the trucks and two rank 'kids' in the form of an ADHD Jack Russell and a paranoid Pomeranian cross that had a nervous bladder condition. And, of course, she had Brian. A grumpy forty-something-year-old husband, who, no matter how many lingerie outfits she bought from Bras N Things, wouldn't make love to her. Or if she did finally talk him into it, she'd be left lying in a pool of no-use semen, feeling empty from his lacklustre performance and cold distance. He'd grumble that the 'no kids factor' was to do with her being too skinny and having tits like two tiny mozzie bites.

'Fuckin' kid'd starve with those things,' he'd say, pointing at her chest.

But Celia knew different. She'd make a good mum. And the doctor's tests said otherwise. It was Brian, for sure, who was the dud stud.

When she saw the fifty-kilometre marker, Celia felt relief seep through her that her day was almost over. She was looking forward to a shower, even though she recalled the motel bathroom had grimy checkerboard-patterned tiling in it. The kind that made you feel you needed to wear thongs and have another wash after standing behind the slimy plastic curtain with the small rounds of soap that looked and smelled like they belonged in men's urinals. Maybe, Celia thought hopefully, they had renovated the motel bathrooms since her last stopover there. But she doubted it.

Celia rolled her eyes. She loved the trucks and the lifestyle they offered, if you could call any of it 'style'. But, at the same time, she hated the trucks. All the driving gave her too much time to think, especially after reading a certain erotic novel she'd bought from the supermarket and the conversations with her friends that had followed. Thank god they didn't yet have the books out on audio for the trucker blokes to buy. It would cause a double-lane pile-up for sure, if they listened to it and drove the big rigs at the same time.

After gossiping about the books with her women friends, Celia had discovered most of her girlfriends were quite different to her when it came to sex with their husbands. Most pretended to be asleep each time their men woke with a 'morning glory', or others would only 'pay their husband with the hairy cheque book' in return for new clothes or a trip to the Gold Coast in winter. It was after those gossipy talks that Celia realised she was different. She was always gagging for it. On that score, she and Brian had been mismatched from the start. Even in the early days of their marriage, Brian was slacker than a Brahman steer's pizzle when it came to bedroom action. He'd sooner wash the truck or suck on a smoke than put in a bit of effort in the sack. It took all Celia's powers of persuasion to coax a quick shag from him on the lounge on a Saturday arvo during the footy half-time.

Celia sighed a long tired sigh that matched the sudden gushing release of her air brakes as she stopped the engine in the truck washbay. When she opened the door, she was hit with an intense blast of Queensland heat. It was a bit much for a Victorian, she thought. As she felt the burn of the concrete rise up through the soles of her steel-capped boots, she glanced around. There was one truck parked in the other washbay and clearly the driver was having a kip in the sleeper. Otherwise it was quiet. It was obviously a non-sale day — not one beast in the yards. Not a soul in sight.

She hauled off her 'Brian's Transport Service' polo top and flicked it up into the cab. Wearing cut-off denim shorts that were vastly on the skimpy side and her white Bonds singlet, Celia went to find the high-pressure hose and try to work out the fancy credit-card swipe system. What did it matter she was wearing no bra? She had no tits anyway, as Brian constantly reminded her.

She stood with one hip jutting out and studied the payment instructions on the washbay machine. It was all Greek to her, no matter how many times she read the step-by-step instructions. She tapped the credit card on her bottom lip and frowned at the machine, muttering at it.

The silence was shattered when Celia heard the vibrating throb of the next washbay pump kick in and a solid jet of water hit the metal sides of the other truck nearby. She glanced over.

'Smart bastard,' she said, envious that that trucker had his hose on the go.

After a few more swipes and a few more button-punchings, there was still no response. Buggered if she could get the thing working. She thought she'd better go ask for help while there was someone about at the deserted saleyards.

Walking to the rear of the big B-double, she eyed the Northern Territory plates on the giant International. Judging from the smell, and the soupy slops that were running from the stock crate's metal sides onto the concrete and through the metal grille of the drainage system, the truck had just carted cattle. She was about to call out 'Hello' when a jet of water as powerful as a cannon hit her full force in the chest. Gasping, she saw beyond the spray a thickset man. He stepped back with a look of utter surprise on his face. Then a look of apology ran to his expression when he saw he had hit a woman full force with his hose. He quickly mouthed 'Sorry' as he pointed the nozzle away from her, the jets of water juddering up from the concrete, casting mini-rainbows into the air.

Celia was about to give him what-for when she realised the blast of water was a welcome relief from the heat and actually felt bloody good ... a bit friggin' hard, but good. And he had looked really funny with that 'Oh, shit!'

expression on his face. She began to giggle as she realised they both must've looked equally funny. Then Celia began to laugh. She swiped her bleached-blonde hair from her forehead and walked over to the man. She could see the relief in him as he looked at her laughing face.

'Sorry, love,' he said, chuckling and grimacing at the same time, comically. 'Didn't see you there. Honest.'

He had to shout over the jet blasts spurting from the water gun. Celia took in his bull-like neck and short-cropped dark hair. He wore a faded blue singlet and jeans. He was so stocky the legs of his jeans folded over on themselves and pooled in a ripple of cuffs at his lace-up work boots. Steel caps, she noticed, like hers. She sucked in a breath. Maybe it was the cold water? Maybe the heat of the day? Maybe the stretch of broken white lines and hot bitumen she'd just travelled? But there was something utterly sexy about him. She continued to smile.

'I just came to ask for a hand,' she shouted over the thrumming pump, 'with the credit card.' She thumbed in the direction of her washbay.

He nodded and smiled, his eyes roving to her erect nipples that were clearly showing through her singlet. When she realised, shocked, he could see every bit of her breasts, she felt blood gush to her cheeks and then, uncontrollably, to her pussy.

'I'll be right with you, love,' he said. 'I'm on a timer, so just let me finish up here.'

'Sure,' she said. 'Wish we'd had a camera. That would've made it on to *Australia's Funniest Home Videos.*'

Then she turned and left him to his uncontrollable smiling and the task of hosing out his Inty. As she walked away, she also took from him the haunting feeling of a desire so powerful she could feel her wet nipples burn and tingle.

As Celia went back to her truck, she looked down at her clinging wet singlet, which was already starting to warm in the evening heat. She glanced back at the man. He didn't know she was watching, but she saw him reach down to adjust the erection that was very obvious in the jeans he was wearing. He saw her looking and, with embarrassment, quickly turned away.

Suddenly a rampaging desire flooded her fully. Shielded now by the giant cliff-sides of her truck, Celia shut her eyes and hopped from one foot to the other in a dance of frustration. If she didn't come in her pants soon, she thought she would die. All those months of pent-up tension. All those months and months of nothingness.

She thought of the man at the truck and his strong broad shoulders. His big handsome belly. And, mostly, his eyes roaming over her body as if she was as tasty as a chicken Wing Ding. She thought about the erection that she had caused. *She had caused!* She leaned her back against the side of the truck, feeling the hot steel press into her wet skin. Desperate, breathing hard, she hastily undid the top button of her shorts and shoved her hand down the front of her pants. Then she buried a finger deep inside her hot wet vagina and gasped with relief, just to feel her own sex. With her other hand, she grappled at her breasts. It didn't take her long to find her rhythm. She was stunned at how wet she was. How soft and pliable her sex was. Her fingers weren't enough. More, she thought, she was desperate for more. As she fingered herself and pressed the fleshy mound at the base of her thumb onto her clitoris, she felt herself on the brink of climax. Her thigh muscles tight. Her head pounding. Her back pressed hard against the pungent, rich-smelling stock crate. The sky contracting in her vision. Her one aim was to come. To explode the feeling of imprisonment from her tightly wound body. She opened her mouth and rubbed faster. Harder. Almost there.

But at that moment the man appeared around the side of the truck's cab. A look of shock passed instantly across his face. His expression morphed again into embarrassment, but before he turned away, Celia recognised in his eyes that same wave of desire. Hastily she pulled her hand from her shorts, did the button up and walked after him. He had his back to her, making his way to his truck.

'Bloody wedgie,' she said with blokey bravado. 'Been shitting me since the Gold Coast. Sorry 'bout that. Don't know who invented G-strings. Silly idea.' Her cheeks were flame red. So were his. She stood breathing hard before him. A silent pulse of time between them. Her eyes softened. The loneliness washed through her again. The weariness of her life.

'You asked for a hand?' he said gently, his voice quavering a little. He did nothing now to hide the wanting in him and the way his penis pressed tight against the fabric of his jeans.

'Yes. I'd love a hand.'

'And whereabouts would you like this hand?' His voice carried the heavy weight of sexual suggestion, but also a dryness of humour, and Celia noted a tone of kindness. His eyes passed over her breasts and looked down at her crutch. Celia realised he hadn't bought the wedgie line. He knew what she had been doing. She decided to play the haughty card. God knows she'd needed it many times on the trucking route, where some of the driving men were as sleazy as some nightclub bouncers or professional football players.

Celia tossed her head in the air like a right snob. 'You should know I'm married,' she said with finality, and walked back to the truck washbay.

The man merely smiled and followed her. 'Married or not, you sure could do with a hand, my lady.'

She shut her eyes and held back both tears and an uprising of laughter. Could it have got any more embarrassing? He was going to give this one a good whirl when he got back in the truck and on the UHF radio to his mates. She'd be the talk of Brisbane's trucking airwaves. She sighed.

'Here,' he said, 'like this … step one …'

Celia barely took in his instruction as he showed her how to insert the card and press the buttons. She only noticed how near he stood so their heads were bent close together. The scent of him was a relaxant and, at the same time, was spinning her into another inner frenzy of wanting.

'Bob's your uncle,' he said after the screen flashed 'Approved' and the high-pressure hose suddenly came throbbing to life.

'Got a bit of kick!' he yelled as he pointed the water gun at the truck. The jets hitting the metal sides of the stock crate set up a tinging and thrumming that sounded like a helicopter or two flying past low. Celia looked at him and mouthed 'Thank you'.

'Best to put it on a lower setting and soak the dung first … then you get to the froth, and last, the high pressure.' He flicked the dial and the pulse of water lowered to a bubbling jet stream. Celia ran her hand under it.

'It's nice and cool.'

'You want me to wet you again?' he asked, letting the hose pulse at the foot of her boots.

'You've wet me all over,' she said, 'inside and out.'

'I could see that. I'll wet you again, darlin', if you want.'

'Could you? Would you? Again?'

Next he was pointing the hose at Celia's chest, a big gorgeous Aussie-boy grin on his face, the water coaxing her nipples erect again. He had nice teeth, she noticed. Good enough to be in a toothpaste commercial.

He circled the hose around each pert little breast, then slowly drew the jet of water lower to her crutch, his eyes holding hers in a gaze of desire. She looked to his jeans and saw his erect knob still pressing outwards, the outline of the head of his penis obvious. The sight of it caused her pussy to pulse. She saw him looking there, to her crutch. The embarrassment washed away between them both.

With one hand, he reached down and undid the button of his jeans and let the zipper fall. His erection sprang from his underpants and there in the glowing Queensland light

Celia feasted her eyes on the largest, most majestic cock she had ever seen. A prize catch after Brian's tiddler. Her eyes lit up at the sight. She smiled in appreciation and her mouth fell open with wanting.

She pressed her back up against the tyre of the truck and spread her legs. The hard jets of water he fired at her pulsed against her clitoris. It felt delicious through the fabric of her denim shorts. She watched the water froth and spurt from the nozzle of the gun and felt herself rushing towards the peak of climax. A climax she thought she must have, now, otherwise she might die. She looked to the man with his cock in his hand. He was tugging on his own beautiful dick, his legs cast in a wide stance, his eyes on her tits, standing just a metre away from her. She saw in him desire for her. Desire for *her*! The realisation washed through her body with pleasure. The man raised the hose to just the right point on her body. The jet of water pulsed with the movement of his hands. Celia cried out in climax and just as she did she heard the man do the same. She saw his penis buck and tense in his hand. A spurt of semen gushed upwards in a perfect arc and she felt the warmth of the white vibrant liquid land on her chest just as the last waves of her own orgasm shuddered through her.

Both of them stood for a time, catching their breath, a smile in their eyes. He hosed her some more, then turned the hose on himself before doing up his jeans.

'Thanks,' she said eventually.

'A pleasure, madam. Where you headed?' he asked, his mouth as sexy as a summer's night.

'North. And you?' she asked.

'South,' he said.

'A pity,' she said.

He shrugged. 'I'm running late, sorry. But I'm sure I'll see you round, pretty lady.' He came over to her, kissed her lightly on the cheek.

Celia nodded and smiled up at him. The man smiled down at her, then he began to walk away.

'Thanks again for the help with the wash,' she said.

He turned and blew her a kiss. She watched him leave, trying to hold in her memory every detail of him. His wide shoulders, his muscled legs, the back of his square head, the way his square hands swung from ultra-strong arms as he walked. She photographed every bit of it in her mind, even bottling the memory of the scent of him and the sound of the spurting water and their combined gasps of pleasure.

Celia hugged herself and cast her head to the sky in bliss with a smile as wide as the horizon. Then she waited as he fired up the engine and watched him and the B-double truck and trailer rattle out of the washbay and turn onto the big old highway. After he had rolled out of sight, his brake lights winking at her on the bend, Celia swiped her credit card and with a grin, turned the hose on herself again.

Rodeo Clown

$\mathcal{D}$riving her little green bubble car, Anne Boxright turned into the Tunbamboola Twilight Rodeo grounds and stopped at the gate, where one of two rather frumpy-looking women in high-vis vests trundled over from the shade of a canopy tent.

Anne jabbed off the air-conditioning, turned down her favourite indie rock band, the Yeah Yeah Yeahs, who were playing from her iPhone through the car stereo, and wound the window down.

'Fifty dollars for the weekend,' one of the women said in a broad accent, 'or fifteen dollars just for this arvo and the band tonight.'

'Fifty bucks!' answered Anne. 'That's a bit steep. I'm here on a uni assignment. I'm a student. Can I get in for free?' Anne had barely had enough money for fuel for the drive here. She'd blown her last student payment buying some eccy at a nightclub and was still paying for it in other ways. After her all-nighter and the buzz she no longer remembered, the world still seemed a little weird and she felt a whole lot poorer in every way.

The high-vis woman turned to her mate. 'Shirl, this here's a uni student. Can she come in for free?'

The woman, who Anne now knew as Shirl, waddled over in her sensible navy shoes and lavender tracksuit and top. The woman surveyed Anne's pale skinny arms and her bobbed black hair and fringe that was cut in a dead-straight line across her pixie-like serious face. Shirl then took time to stare at her cream, see-through, draped-crepe top with black sailor-boy collar and matching black buttons.

'A student, eh? I can see you're not from round here. What are you studyin', darl?'

Anne almost rolled her eyes. She didn't want to get stuck here talking to two old crones who couldn't apply lipstick properly, had haircuts like road workers, and clothes that looked as if they were bought from the specials racks at Best & Less. She sighed.

'Sociology, anthropology and environmentalism. You know,' Anne said with boredom in her tone.

'Is that right?' said Shirl. 'In-ter-esting. And what brings you to the Tunbamboola Rodeo?'

'Oh, just the assignment.'

'And what assignment would that be, darl?'

'An anthropological study on male aggression.'

'Male aggression?' Shirl looked perplexed. 'Bull males? Or human males?'

'It's *anthropology*,' Anne said as if spelling the word out to a simple person. '*Human* male aggression.'

'You won't find much human male aggression round here, but anyways suit yourself. If you want in, you can have in.' Then the woman paused, narrowed her eyes and said slowly, 'You're not from one of those animal activity mobs, are you, sweetheart? Coz if you are, the rodeo folk said if any one of youse turn up, they're happy to give you a cuppa and a tour of the back chutes and a chance to meet the riders and animals. Bulls and all. I'm not that into rodeos meself, just here for the Ladies Guild, but I do love animals. I'm very good to my animals … in fact, my dog —'

'No! I'm not here about animals!' Anne interrupted. 'I'm just doing an anthropological assignment, like I told you. I've got an interview with …' Anne looked across to her notes that were sitting on the passenger seat of the car, 'a … Randy Carter from the Rodeo Association.'

The older women exchanged knowing glances.

'Ooh! Randy!' Both of them chuckled and nodded in what looked like appreciation and admiration for the man.

'He'll be happy to chat to a pretty little thing like you.' Shirl grinned with her badly capped teeth. Then the other woman piped up.

'Randy's working flat out, darling, with the rodeo. And he won't be done till dark. Then he's got to water and feed his horses and all. You'd best get the weekend ticket, if I was you. Catch up with him first thing in the morning, before the Professional Bareback.' She shook her head. 'Tonight'll be too noisy when the band's on, to interview anyone. Those Wolfe Brothers really do crank it up for us.'

Still offended by being called 'a pretty little thing', Anne shook her head and sighed. These women truly were simple.

'Fine. So, how much for my entry?' Anne asked.

Shirl scratched her jagged short grey hair with thick, chunky fingers.

'Well, dear, the proceeds of the gate fees go to the local respite care … if you'd like to make a contribution, just a donation, we can let you in on student rates.'

'And how much would that be?' Anne said, getting really hot under her sailor's collar.

'Whatever you can spare, duck.'

Anne fished around in the ashtray of her car and passed the lady a couple of two-dollar coins, then looked distastefully at the program that the woman handed her. It had the silhouette of a cowboy riding a bucking horse.

'Thank you for your generosity,' the woman said, smiling but with a hint of piss-take in her tone. 'You've missed the broncs, darl. But you may be in time for the roping. Enjoy yourself and your studyin'.'

'Right. Thanks,' Anne said, wondering if all country people were that slow. She accelerated away, driving on to where rows and rows of country cars and utes were parked. Her little car lumped and thumped its way over the rough-mown, clumpy pasture. Anne grimaced with each jolt. Then she grimaced some more when she saw some redneck rodeo patrons passing by in frayed jeans and shorts, boots and checked shirts and cowboy hats. It was all so predictable. The people looked hostile. Like fringe-dwellers.

'So uncool,' she muttered to herself.

She really wished her roommate, Sally, had come with her, but Sally was living it up at a rave somewhere out on the eastern side of the city. Sally didn't like the country. It was too uncouth for her. Even Anne's boyfriend, Simon, had passed on coming with her on the trip, despite her offering to pay for a motel room. He had said he was busy with his computer networking thesis, but Anne knew he would be going to see Eddie, and his housemates, to spend the weekend drinking beers and playing stupid computer games.

She could picture (and smell) the wobbly-gutted Eddie now, sitting in his tip of a bedroom, while her pale, thin boyfriend, Simon, would be plugged into his laptop in the lounge room, blinking behind his glasses. The other housemates, Skeet and Thommo, would be in on it too, isolated in their own rooms, but linked into the same virtual reality game via wi-fi. They were games involving warriors and bomb making and the boys were obsessed with them.

Early in their relationship, Anne would go with Simon to Eddie's and sit at Simon's feet reading her books while he played on the computer. But the male testosterone that lurked in the house, the smell of boy farts and lack of sunlight started to get to her. She discovered early on it was best to leave Simon to it when he was gaming.

As she got out of her car, she felt the heat of the afternoon wrap around her. She tugged down her high-waisted black pencil skirt and kicked a grass seed off the top of her dainty little foot, which was encased by delicate red cloth-covered flats, trimmed with tiny black bows. She grabbed for her natural-fibre woven overseas-aid bag from the front seat, which contained her pad and pen, and picked up her iPhone so as to record this so-called 'U.S. rodeo star'. As she locked her car, she felt apprehension gather in her. She was about to throw herself into this very male and brutish domain of animal cruelty and machismo.

As Anne walked around a big corrugated shed, she was met with a sight she hadn't been expecting. The rodeo ground was shaded by large leafy trees and beneath them sat groups of people on beautiful green lawns. Mostly families on picnic blankets. There were cowboy-type dads pushing strollers, young girls lying in the sun in cut-off jeans and kids running about, their faces painted, balloons in hand. Mums sat chatting or passing food to their kids. Up in the stand were more clusters of families, all wearing hats against the brightness and heat of the summer afternoon, watching the dusty space of the arena that lay before them surrounded by high metal railings.

Gingerly Anne sidestepped up the scaffold seating in her rather restrictive skirt and sat. With a sudden burst, gates clanged open below. A calf sprang from nowhere. Two riders pelted out twirling ropes and within seconds, before the dust even had time to rise, they had lassoed a little horned steer the colour of caramel slice. The horses stood stock-still, keeping the ropes taut, the cowboys leaping off and hitching the calf, the crowd thundering applause like rain and the commentator revving the show along with an excited twang.

Anne wasn't sure what she had just seen, but as the men let the little calf up again, she watched as it shook the dust from its coat. It instantly cast its ears forward to the gate where its friends were waiting. Calmly the calf trotted back from whence it had come. The men ambled back over to their horses, took up the split reins, smoothed grateful gloved hands down the perfectly muscled necks of their well-trained mounts, stepped back into their saddles and, like the calf, calmly walked their horses from the arena. As the announcer introduced the next roping pair, Anne looked about. She wondered which of the cowboys around the ground might be Randy Carter.

'Hat, love?' came a voice beside her.

She turned to see a middle-aged woman with two freckled redhead kids sitting beside her. 'Pardon?'

'Would you like a hat? I've got a spare,' the woman said, offering up a cap with *Darren's Stock Transport* embroidered on it. 'Wouldn't want to see that pretty little face of yours get burnt.'

Anne frowned. What was it with these people and the 'pretty little' line? She shook her head. 'No. I'm fine, thank you.'

'Not in an hour you won't be. I suggest you sit in the shade, if you're not gunna wear a hat. This sun will sting that lovely pale skin of yours.'

Anne tugged the skirt down over her white knees and looked at the woman as if she was an irritating insect. 'You wouldn't happen to know where I'd find Randy Carter, would you?'

The woman laughed. 'Randy Carter! Ha! Why sure I know where to find him. Every woman knows where to find Randy.'

'Yes, but where would *I* find him?' Anne asked, hot and irritated.

The woman looked at Anne for a moment, her head tilted quizzically to the side, as if she was reading something about her. Eventually she said, after a subtle lift of her eyebrows, 'Round the back of the bull chutes, I expect. But he's on after this. He won't be done until at least after five. I reckon you're gunna have to wait.'

Anne sighed and stood up. She had to find some water. As she went to leave, the woman called after her, 'My pleasure, love. No worries.'

Bull riding was the last event of the day and Anne, who was now lobster pink, stood beneath one of the giant elms, feeling her skin pulling taut painfully from sunburn. The noise from the bar was lifting. She was hoping to witness some rodeo male aggression there, but so far the lads and older men stood chatting in a friendly manner, stopping every now and then to watch the arena events. A buzz seemed to rise when the bulls were let up into the chutes and cowboys in white hats and tight safety vests emerged on the rail.

Anne couldn't help but notice the fitness of the men. Their fringed leather chaps opened up to denim in the crutch area at the front, and at the back highlighted perfect denim-clad backsides. Every one of the cowboys seemed to have on a colourful shirt with Wrangler written on the sleeve or back. And each had spurs and dusty white hats that curved upwards at the sides. She had to swallow down a feeling that the men looked sexy. Really sexy. But in an aggressive over-the-top masculine way. Not like Simon who wore slip-on shoes, with long shorts and, mostly pilling, polo tops he bought from the op shop. He preferred to spend his money on computer games than clothing.

Over the loudspeaker, country rock music cranked loudly, the strains of a maniac harmonica blared and deep thumping drums kicked out a Garth Brooks tune as the first gate was swung and a bull rocked from the crush. On the giant black beast's back sat the most athletic man Anne had ever seen. He was flung this way and that, one arm cast back high in the air, the other clutching a rope around the bull's neck. She wondered for a moment if that was Randy Carter. She hadn't caught the commentator's call. She was feeling a little giddy. Then she heard a bell ring and a cheer rise up from the crowd. She watched as a man who had been standing behind a colourful barrel sprinted towards the beast and leaped in front of the big horned bull. He was dressed as a clown and darted this way and that as another clown dived in to help unhook the rider who was clearly stuck fast to the binding on the bull's rigging and was getting tossed about like a rag doll. It looked rough. It looked dangerous. It looked … and it was at that point, Anne fainted.

When she woke, Anne found herself on a St John Ambulance stretcher bed, with the doors of the cab wide open, revealing the leafy canopy of the shady trees. Above her was a red-faced man and a pimply young woman.

'Where's your hat, young lady?' said the man.

'What?'

'Heatstroke.'

'But ...'

'Don't worry, love. Someone's gone to find Randy. They said he was a friend of yours.'

'Randy?' Anne said, sitting up and feeling woozy, knowing that it was more than just heatstroke that had caused her to faint. After another fight with Simon she'd partied pretty hard this week. Memories of her drug-fuelled rave came back to haunt her. She was still toxed. She knew it.

At that moment, at the back of the vehicle, the rodeo clown she saw earlier appeared. He wore runners, bright red skins that showed off perfectly formed legs, big oversized denim shorts held up with yellow braces and a pink shirt with large stars of various colours splashed over it. Rags of green, yellow and red hung from his belt and beneath his dusty cowboy hat was a riotous red curling wig. His face was painted, smeared with white, a big red clown mouth turned upwards and he had the signature black smudges above and below the white circles of his clown eyes.

'Randy, hi!' said the pimply girl in the tone of an airhead, Anne thought.

'Why hello, Darlene,' he said in a slow southern American accent.

'Thanks for visiting my brother in hospital last week,' the spotty St John volunteer said, her eyes illuminated with an obvious display of girlie crush.

'My pleasure. He's a cute kid. I hope he's feelin' better.' Randy turned to look at Anne. 'So, they tell me you're the lass from the uni, come to grill me?'

'I ...?' Anne began, embarrassed to be found in an ambulance by her interviewee. She swung her legs over the side of the bed, just as the St John man stepped forward with a rehydration drink for her.

'Sit up slowly, young lady. We don't want you cracking your scone if you faint again.'

Randy surveyed her from behind his clown make-up and shook his head. 'No point you interviewing me in your present state. You'd better come back to my camp. Have a bit of a rest. Thank you, Darlene, thank you, Frank. I can take the little lady from here.'

A while later Anne found herself with a thumping headache at Randy's 'camp', which was an extremely long horse trailer he called a Gooseneck. Inside were angled bays for the horses, where a big palomino stood munching on hay. Randy had sat her in a deck chair and showed her where he cooked, ate, slept and showered, which was basically in the back of the truck with the horses.

'It's charming,' she said sarcastically. 'And why isn't this poor horse out in the yards with the others? Why is he shut in here?' Anne turned to look at the strangely dressed man before her. It was hard to tell his age through the face paint. It was hard to tell his body shape. He had protective gear under his shirt and just looked boxy and square.

'Mostly coz he likes it in here with me. We're pretty good mates and because he's a bull.'

'A bull? But he's a horse,' Anne said.

Randy laughed. 'I mean he's a bull. He's a stallion,' he said. 'You want to know about male aggression, little lady? He'll kill another male that gets between him and his girls.'

Anne looked at the placid horse with the golden mane that looked as if it belonged in a Disney video. 'Really?'

'Ma'am, with all due respect, you don't know much about animals and men, do ya?'

Anne felt herself stiffen. She was dux of her year last year at uni and had scored distinctions right the way through this semester. And she had a boyfriend.

She was about to answer when Randy, who was chewing on the end of a bit of hay, said, 'Why do you think we castrate most of the male animals in our farming systems? It's to keep order. That many males and all that testosterone would be too hard to handle. If you had seen them bulls out there today, you would've realised that running one thousand of those boys in one herd together would create all kinds of hell-raising. That's kinda what's happened to humans on planet Earth. There are a lot of males out there should never been bred, causing wars and pollution and a whole world of trouble. In farming, we leave the nuts in the best of them, the calm ones, the handsome ones, the most productive ones. You cut the nuts out of the rest, because that way you have order and a nice line of animals. I reckon there'd be plenty of women like to do the same to humanity. No use it being a "man's

Rodeo Clown

world" when the men ain't payin' attention to what the women want.'

Anne tried to take in what he was saying. Her head was still thumping.

'Way you come across in the world, ma'am, I reckon you'd like to castrate the aggressive, useless males and select the ones you women want and need for breeding.'

'Excuse me? No! I ...' Anne said, her cheeks flaming red with offence.

'Of course, I can say that confidently, about the castration, because I know the women would keep me as a bull. Not many women wouldn't want babies outta me.'

Anne's mouth dropped open and her eyes widened. The arrogance of the man! 'Why ... you ...!'

She was about to stand up, but Randy had already ducked out of the Gooseneck. When he returned, he handed her a packet of painkillers and a pannikin of what smelled like rum.

'Wash it down with that and it'll all seem better, darlin'. And you do know, I'm teasin' ya. You look like you could do with a bellyachin' laugh.'

'Don't you darlin' me,' Anne said. 'It's patronising.'

'Patronising? Or flatterising?' he said with his clownish grin. 'Now, if you'll excuse me, I need to take a shower. I'm stiff, I'm sore, I'm busted and I'm dusted. This make-up is annoying the hollerin' hell outta me.' And with that, the rodeo clown began to take off his runners and proceeded to undress right there in front of Anne.

'I ... You ... Um, excuse me?' she stammered.

He stopped unbuttoning his shirt and looked at her. Anne could see vibrant blue pupils ringed with grey.

'Well, you are in my shower room. You never seen a man's body before? You can sit outside, but the mozzies'll eat you this time of evening. I suggest you stay right there with your headache and look away, young lady. Or you're welcome to jump right in and join me. It's river water pumped from just outside. Makes your hair nice and soft. Might wash away your headache and your sins.'

'Sins?' She rolled her eyes again. This man was frustrating! Arrogant, aggressive and frustrating!

But Anne found she couldn't help sneaking glances as he dropped the denim clown shorts, pulled off the skins and stood just in his shirt, which he had unbuttoned and was now dropping to the floor. The Velcro of his protective vest made loud ripping noises as he peeled it from his body and then slipped off his singlet. Unashamedly he dropped his underpants, turning to the shower bay that was right there in the back of the Gooseneck alongside the small stove and a pile of horse gear and Anne's chair.

Anne's mouth dropped when she saw his male perfection from behind. The broad shoulders were so brown and muscled that as he reached for the taps she could see the mechanics of his divine body beneath his skin. The way his waist tapered into narrow white buttocks that topped muscled thighs, sculpted as perfectly as the statue of David. Across his back and his side were red welts and bruising. Along his knee she saw a deep red scar that ran in an arc down his shin.

Rodeo Clown

'Why do you do it to your body? Why do rodeo?'

'Why do people base jump?' he said, scrubbing soap onto his chest. 'Why do people race cars? Or surf giant waves?'

'Males seeking mindless adrenaline, through egotistical risk-taking,' she answered.

'Not only males. *You* take risks.'

'I do not.'

'Why do you risk your life taking them dangerous party drugs? Why do you jeopardise that tiny little body of yours that's no bigger than a widget and your busy brain that's too noisy to think straight?'

She sat up, surprised at his question, insulted by his comments.

He ducked under the spray of the shower and began to soap his legs, turning his head to her. Waiting for an answer. She saw the colours of his clown face run in rivulets down his tanned body.

'How do you know I take drugs?'

He began to scrub his face with a flannel, and she watched his shoulder blades move beneath his smooth skin.

'Your eyes are dulled by something, and it isn't the hardship of life. You're as spoiled as Paris Hilton. Nope. You take them drugs. I can read it in your energy. You ain't balanced.'

'Oh, great. Judged by a clown. What would you know about my energy?'

'It's aggressive for one thing,' he said in his southern drawl. 'And your energy is all prickly like.'

'Are you trying to talk metaphysics with me?' she said, flabbergasted by this strange conversation she was having with a naked rodeo clown.

'Would it surprise you if I was? How else does a rodeo protection athlete do his job? We have to know a bit of kinesiology, a bit of quantum physics, a bit of ethology so we can read the bull. How else do we keep ourselves and the bull rider alive unless by knowledge of energetics and our own intuition so we can keep two steps ahead of the bull? And on the ranch, how else does a cowboy gauge the movement of a herd of cattle or the inner ways, the emotions, of his horse? It's all energetics. With some critters, the softer you are, the more powerful you are.'

'Then why torment those poor bulls and horses?'

'Torment! Those animals are bred for it, trained for it, fed and conditioned for it. They are athletes too. They have long lives, long careers and they love it. You can't make a bull buck, same as you can't make a horse buck. You've no doubt heard the expression that you can lead a horse to water, but you can't make it drink. It's the same with this game. If they don't want to do it, they just don't do it. But the animals that do want to do it, they're chasin' the same rush as us. We're a team, them animals and us.'

'I don't need to hear your pro-rodeo spiel,' she said, realising she'd been staring at his buttocks and back for a long time. She took another big slug of rum. 'I'm just here to ask questions for my assignment.'

'Well, that's a shame,' Randy said, turning to face her as the water streamed over his toned body. 'I thought I could've changed your mind about aggression in men. Most of us cowboys are gentle types. Gentle with horses, gentle with women. Family men.'

When Anne saw his face for the first time clean of make-up, she almost fainted again. He was so good-looking, so beautiful, it felt to Anne as if she had looked into the eyes of a god. Cleaned of the face paint, Randy had looks that stole hearts. His skin was smooth and tanned, his jet-black hair framed a manly square-jawed face, his teeth were white and perfect and his sensuous mouth was now moving into a slowly evolving grin.

'I don't mean to be rude, Miss Boxright, but if you stay at university too long, you'll forget about real life. And you may miss your calling as a mother.'

'Excuse me!' she said, red-faced, and angry yet again at this arrogant, yet incredibly delectable, man before her.

'You use this too much,' Randy said, tapping his temple with an index finger. 'When you don't get around animals much, lots of folk forget *they* are animals. You are an animal, and you gotta go with your instincts as the female of the species, not against them.'

'My instinct is not to have children yet ... I've got a whole ...'

'Would your instinct be to hop into this shower with me, as an animal, say, not as a woman, a student and a feminist? As an animal?'

'No, it certainly would not!' she said.

'That's a shame. You might only have fifty eggs to lay.'

'Pardon? Fifty eggs to lay?'

'That's all you might have left inside there.' He gestured to her stomach region. 'So if I were you, I'd be gettin' in touch with your animal instincts. Can you get me a beer, by the way? I wanna wash my hair. If you're feelin' fine to stand and all.'

As Anne got up and reached for a beer out of the tiny fridge, she felt anger simmering within her. She knew he was teasing her. She knew he was playing her. A cowboy as good-looking as him, and clearly as smart as him, could get any woman he wanted.

She thought of Simon, of his spindly legs and flaccid computer-geek arms. His glasses that had fogged when they first kissed. The way he liked to tie her up and hit her with his computer cords. He was weird with sex. She had thought it might grow to be fun, but as time went on, Anne had found herself withering within as a woman. As a lover. No amount of academic reading or study on the matter seemed to ease or help the situation.

'I have a boyfriend, you know,' she said defensively.

'That's just a social construct,' Randy said. 'You know back in the day when we all lived in caves, women mated with many men, at the same time. That's why nowadays men are visually stimulated by watching copulation, because essentially, we are all still animals. It was the strongest sperm that the female was after, so to get a whole bunch of it from different males meant the strongest would fertilise her egg. Mother Nature helping human survival. And, I'm tipping, it's the same today. If women were more like animals and forgot about the money and what life is supposed to be according to the TV, they'd pick the kinder males for most of their love action.'

'And where on the rodeo circuit did you come up with your ingenious anthropological insights, Mr Carter?'

'You're not the only one who is university educated, ma'am, with respect,' he said with a quick tilt of his head and a lift of one eyebrow.

As she handed Randy the beer, their hands touched. She felt water splash onto the front of her top and she looked down to see that the lace bra beneath was clearly showing through.

'You're very pretty,' Randy said, 'and I'm going to embarrass myself in this here shower if you don't turn that lovely face of yours away along with those two pretty lady thangs.'

She looked at him with her deep brown angry eyes. 'Getting all male on me, are you? And what about my prickly energy … you happy to fuck that too?'

'There's no need to be coarse and hostile now, Anne,' Randy said, sipping calmly on his beer. 'I can see what's within you. You're like a scared filly that keeps laying her ears back at the world and threatening to kick. Once you find your place of love and lose the fear, you'll learn to look at the world with your ears forward, gal. And you'll learn the words "thank you". You're a rare creature. And a beautiful one at that. Worth educatin', I'd say.'

Her present mind flashed insult and anger, but beneath the surface flashed disappointment in herself. In her disasters with men. Her anguished relationship with

Simon. His distant, cold ways once he was unplugged from the violence of his virtual reality games. She felt she had been lost in the world of drug-induced nights in clubs, along with other sweating unhinged souls, lost in the facades of materialism. But here before her was perhaps the toughest, rudest, yet most peaceful, gentle man she had ever met. She felt a tiny crack in her armour.

'And how would you suggest I find my place of love? Through some southern-drawling Jesus church, like you clearly have?'

Anne felt Randy grasp her tiny wrist.

'Our capacity to love is all we truly have,' he said. He pulled her under the jets of the shower and began to kiss her. With a hunger like no other, Anne began to kiss him back. Desperately she helped him peel the sodden shirt from her, reefing off her skirt, dragging down her lace panties, unhooking her bra until she stood naked. The water caressed the skin of her hot, fearful body, washing away the stress of the day and softening her to this foreign world that was such a contrast to the rush and bustle of her life in the city. The *aggressive* rush and bustle of the city, she realised now, that man-made concrete world of commerce and consumerism. She was swamped by it.

Not like here, this dozing place of summertime and countryside, where Mother Nature ruled and there was a peacefulness even in the midst of a jostling rodeo ring. Coarse and rough maybe sometimes, but Anne had seen there was a steady, polite and caring rhythm in the people, a calmness in the animals and a grounding presence from the land. It was all so much more gentle than where she was from.

Pressing herself against Randy's torso, Anne felt his gentle hands roving over her skin. There was a sureness to his touch and with it, she felt every nerve in her body settling. Yielding to him, like she'd seen the horses yield. Big strong men reining their beautifully educated horses around with the softest of imperceptible cues, like a male dancer leading his partner in a waltz.

Randy's lips were full and soft, and his tongue inside her mouth felt warm and sensual. His hands reached for the shower gel and pumped a dollop of pearl liquid onto his palm. Still kissing her, he began to lather the gel over her firm small breasts, and as he did, she felt his knees give a little from the hunger of his own desire. The slide of the lather, the caress of his hands up and over her body, the way he cupped her face, the way he cupped her soft white rounded arse, all made her gasp. A feeling of weakness in her legs from desire overtook her as well, but a feeling of strength in her feminine power suddenly consumed her. She was gone. The thoughts in her head silenced. There was only the beingness of living.

Randy scooped his hand under each of her thighs and, with rock-solid strength, lifted her up and held her, her legs wrapping around him, her hands reaching for the solidity of his firmly muscled shoulders. Then he lowered her onto him. The tip of his large, blood-infused penis dipping in and out of her, slowly at first. Edging in gently, thrust by wanting thrust. Anne couldn't wait though for such a slow entry. She tilted her pelvis, pulled herself down and slammed herself deeply onto the rigid strength of his cock. He was so powerful, his thigh muscles like steel, his tanned biceps like rocks. He moved her up and down with ease, pleasuring himself with her, all the while giving her all she needed in the form of the hardest erection she had ever been blessed to know.

Next she heard him turning off the taps behind her.

'We'll drain the river and flood the campsite at this rate, baby,' he said quietly. 'Come with me.'

Then he stepped from the shower, still inside her, and carried her over to where the horse tack was stored. He dragged down some rugs and horse blankets and gently lay her in the nest of fabric, of summer rugs and coarse cotton-weave saddlecloths. She felt the rough sensation on the skin of her back as he lay on top of her, the sunburn sting barely registering beyond her longing for this cowboy. His horseman hips began to grind against her, so exquisitely slowly, so achingly deliciously, she thought she would die if she couldn't pull him closer, get him to ride her faster.

She cupped her hands around the cheek of each of his pert buttocks and pushed upwards to him, wanting him in every way. He kissed her along the side of her neck, and she shut her eyes and breathed in the smell of horses and working men. He began to ride her faster now, driving into her more firmly and deeply, and she felt the crest of an orgasm build. Lost in a galloping rhythm, she gave in, gave way, gave up and gave to him as her body convulsed in one enormous heave of orgasmic bliss. Then she felt her entire being soften, her whole world soften. Pliable in his hands, he turned her, rolled her onto all fours and pulled her hips and buttocks up to him. In the wet gush of her recent coming, he plunged into her from behind, his hands drawing her to him as he pushed into her.

From beneath the veil of her bobbing fringe, Anne looked up to the end of the Gooseneck trailer. There she saw Randy's golden stallion, his ears pricked forward, his excited gaze in their direction, his head held high. And then Anne saw it, the horse's enormous erection, the mushroom head of his penis inflamed and dripping fluid, bouncing excitedly up against the stallion's belly. The horse didn't shift his hooves. He didn't cry out. Instead, the stallion simply watched.

Anne watched him back. Looking at the giant sex of the animal, feeling like an animal on all fours herself, she gave way to a primeval urge to sap her lover of his semen. She wanted to feel her animal nature that was buried within. She began to flex her buttocks upwards in a rhythm, answering every slam the cowboy gave. The chains of the Gooseneck's dividers began rattling; the whole truck started rocking. She slammed and slammed and slammed against the man behind her and grunted with effort, gritting her teeth. Then she felt the strong clutch of his cowboy grip press into the skin of her rump as he cried out an explosion within her.

Sweating, he draped his body over hers. She kissed the length of his upper arms, their toned perfection. Then Randy rolled onto his back and gently coaxed her to lie in his arms on the horse blankets. He kissed her on her sweating forehead and with a gravelly voice asked if she was alright.

She giggled a girlish giggle. 'I've never been better.'

They lay there for a time, her head on his chest, listening to his heartbeat, its tune a fit and steady rhythm. His was a good heart. This she could feel.

'Tell me the truth,' Randy said eventually, in his mesmerising southern drawl. 'A girl don't learn stuff like that from her mama. You've been reading that naughty book everyone's been goin' on about, haven't ya?'

'I most certainly have not,' Anne said, her tone of offence returning. 'It's not to my literary tastes. Nor feminist ideology. I would never read a book that —' But Randy cut her off mid-sentence.

'Ah, never say never, darlin'! Before today, cowboys weren't your taste. But now you've tried one, you'll want him again.'

'Will I now?' she said, knowing it was true.

'You wanna come back to my farm where I breed the bucking bulls? I can show you some real good beef. Nice animals. Top bulls. Heck, I might even have fifty bulls of grey. How's that grab you?'

She looked over to his manly godsend of a face and for the first time in years Anne laughed properly. From her belly. Without the weight of the world. Without thinking of anything, other than simply feeling gratitude for the bliss, beauty and mystery of life.

'Fifty bulls of grey!' she laughed. 'That's funny! Oh, you clown!'

'Actually, in the industry,' Randy said with a slow and cheeky grin, 'we ain't clowns. We prefer to call ourselves bullfighters. And that's what I do, with people and animals, fight the bull out of them.'

'Is that right?' she said.

'That's right,' he said, winking.

And with that, Anne sank back into his big strong cowboy arms and sighed, realising how long her journey to find this place had been.

The Joining

*I*t came as somewhat of a pleasant shock for Marrilyn Ruthbridge that she was getting banged solidly from behind, doggy-style, by Garry Goodwood, in her home. Both of them were almost fully clothed save for Garry's half-mast trousers and Marrilyn's slightly unbuttoned blouse and rucked-up tweed skirt. Her undergarment of cream bloomers had been hastily tossed away and now lay beneath the chaise.

How this act came to pass was something of a mystery to her, but for now, feeling the happy slap of the gentleman's low-slung balls against her buttocks and sensing the thick smooth skin of his manhood rim in and out of her own surprisingly moistened lady parts, Marrilyn had decided to go with the situation. She glanced sideways beyond the floral couch and out her lounge-room window to the decking where King, her prizewinning trial kelpie, stood, knotted and panting with Garry's bitch, Cindy.

As Garry pumped like a man possessed, Marrilyn decided she was enjoying being on all fours. It was so much nicer than the last time she assumed this bodily position, when she had recently been cleaning the kitchen cupboards. The slate flooring had given her knees hell at the time, but today, her knees felt rather fine on the pure wool carpet … tickety-boo, in fact. It was possibly a decade since her last sexual encounter and Marrilyn had forgotten how vigorous it was. And how much fun.

She was not used to entertaining men in her home either. Certainly not like this! It was only recently that her lovely wisteria-shaded deck outside the lounge room had become a place of canine lovemaking, as kelpie bitches roamed the deck with swollen vulvas, squatting to leave urine and a heady dose of pheromones ready for King to inspect, and later, for Marrilyn to hose away. The men who brought the bitches would make polite bloodlines and breeding chitchat as they sipped from Marrilyn's small teacups, while King humped his way home.

Up until today, Marrilyn thought the men had all come to woo King for the purposes of breeding, not her. But then Garry, the quiet widower, had surprised her with a stammering confession. He had fancied her for the past year on the Yard Dog Trial competition circuit and would she be so kind as to have a meal at the local hotel with him tonight, before he began his journey back to his property in South Australia?

Marrilyn had felt a flash of shyness. But as King and Cindy began to flirt and King mounted Cindy outside the window, Marrilyn felt a sudden rush within her. Garry must have sensed it and had swooped upon Marrilyn, holding her breathlessly and pressing what was a desperate kiss upon her lips. In the past, she would have been shocked, but it had been a lonely few years and Marrilyn was grateful that a fine man like Garry would have deep feelings for her. Her memory flickered through a movie of past encounters with Garry at various Yard Dog competitions at various showgrounds around the country. She recalled Garry bringing her a salad roll during a lunch break, and a paper plate loaded with slice and biscuits during morning tea. On their arrival at the trial grounds he had often walked with her while King emptied out, the dog focused intently on his toileting. The way he had heartily congratulated her with a kiss after she had beaten him and Cindy by three points in the semifinals. His concern each time she put King in the dog crate and started her engine to make the long journey home to Glencraig. She smiled. She hadn't seen it. She hadn't been looking to see.

Now with each thrust from Garry, she noticed the rattling of the glass cabinet containing her fine bone china figurines. The floor shook and the Limited Edition Monica, who carried the flower basket of roses, began to wobble; the delicate woman teetered on the dust-free shelf inside and was rattling her way dangerously close to the Swan Lake ballerina. Suddenly the Limited Edition Monica took a tumble, toppling the ballerina over with a *chink*. That, in turn, brought down the tuxedoed Rhett, who up until a moment ago, had stood in an elegant waltz pose with the equally limited edition '*Gone with the Wind* Scarlett Southern Belle of the Ball'. Marrilyn had set herself a goal of collecting fifty of the figurines before her fiftieth birthday. If one broke now, it would leave her with forty-eight in her collection. Two off target before June.

'Excuse me,' Marrilyn said to Garry. 'Tewwibly sowwy to point this out wight now, but my Woyal Doulton is getting quite upset. Would you mind?' She nodded towards the cabinet.

'Pardon?' said Garry, who momentarily stopped his thrusting and looked towards the oakwood display case. 'Oh, yes. Awfully sorry. Shall we … ah?' He inclined his head in the direction of the dogs outside the French doors.

'Ehm, yes,' she said primly, which she realised was rather an odd tone for her to use, given her situation. 'That would be tewwific. Thank you.' Then Garry and she, still joined, crab-crawled across the rug towards the window, safely away from the figurines. There, in a patch of sunlight, Garry Goodwood gently cupped Marrilyn Ruthbridge's broad horsewoman's hips, and began again to tip his pelvis towards her, in and out, with a punctual beat.

Normally she wouldn't ever have entertained the thought of starting a relationship with a man named Garry. Not that they *were* in a relationship, and not that she had an aversion to his name, although she knew her mother would have. But she had always been careful in her younger years to select boyfriends who carried no 'r' in their name. Not that she'd had many boyfriends. Only one to speak of. Only Hugo.

Back when Marrilyn's parents had christened their baby girl in a Cambridge church, they hadn't known that their child wouldn't ever be able to say her 'r's. Had they known this fact, they would never have named their baby Marrilyn Roweena Ruthbridge.

The issue of Marrilyn's speech had meant a lifetime of avoiding eye contact with people so as not to engage in conversation. It had meant not saying very much at all … especially to Australian boys. Boys who cruelly teased her at her rural school.

'Mawwilyn Woweena Wuthbwidge,' they would taunt. 'Fwom Gweat Bwitain now wesiding in Victowia, Austwalia, on Glencwaig Fawm!' Then they would pretend to ride horses and call out, 'Twot on! Twot on!'

Her adolescence was a disaster. It was easier for Marrilyn to stay out with the poddy lambs and the sheep dogs when Mother entertained the other graziers' wives and their children than to sit and join in. As a result, Marrilyn spent much of her time on the farm with the workmen and Father, or on her pony getting more and more precise in her riding and competitive about beating the popular girls at pony club. She had quite a talent with animals. And Father had taught her about British class and status, so her speech deficit never bothered her around the workmen, because she became a good leader to them. It was only in the world outside Glencraig Estate that she struggled.

Marrilyn's life had been something of a solo journey for her. She had been twelve when she had been shipped out from Britain to the antipodes by her parents, following the death of an Australian-based relative, who owned a rather large estate in Victoria's Western District. The distant uncle was somehow connected to them through the Earl of Dottingtonshire, a somewhat distant line itself, and in a twist of fate, had left his entire farming estate to his sole surviving relative, Marrilyn's father.

For a long time now, Marrilyn had shut herself off from men and had never really been that interested in sexual acts. Mother and Father had never much made mention of the birds and the bees when she was growing up. But lately Marrilyn had noticed everyone seemed to be talking about fornication since questionable books began appearing in supermarkets. Farming folk on the dog trial circuit were even talking about the books. It was unusual that anal fisting was a topic of conversation around the yards, but the books seemed to have prompted such talk. They didn't appeal to Marrilyn at all. Give her a Simone de Beauvoir and D.H. Lawrence any day, she thought. However, if it made people happy, who was she to judge the literary tastes of other grocery shoppers? Live and let live, she had always thought.

Today, though, the feeling of a man being so deep inside and heavy upon her made her think she ought to reconsider her stance on physical liaisons. It was actually really, really rather nice, and not simply for the purpose of reproduction of the human species.

Without a word, Garry suddenly withdrew from her and, using his slim grazier's hands to guide her, encouraged Marrilyn to roll over onto her back, those same hands gently spreading her thin, strong legs. Marrilyn lay still as Garry guided his John Thomas into her once more and she again felt the odd sensation of sexual arousal when he resumed his thrusts in what she knew was the missionary position. This time the cabinet only rattled slightly, the figurines safe from the outside world of vibrations brought on by the sudden copulation. From this new angle, Marrilyn could see the fabric peony-print pelmets of the curtains above her head. They were terribly pretty. But could do with a dust.

'Everything alright, dear?' Garry queried, pausing for a moment, looking down at her from where he was propped above, his tidy striped farm shirt still buttoned almost to his neck, his neatly creased cream slacks and navy underpants trapping his ankles together at his R.M. Williams polished boots. 'Comfortable? Enjoying yourself?'

'Oh, yes! Bwilliant, thank you,' she said. Then, by way of encouragement, she gave him the slightest slap on his bottom as a 'giddy-up' cue to resume his very pleasant gait. He enjoyed this action immensely, judging by his immediate response of strong vocals … made up mostly of wobbly vowels strung together.

'OooOoo OoooooOo! Aeeeiiooouuu! Ouuuuooo!' said Garry.

She slapped him again, a little harder, and extracted an 'AHH!' from him, then kept on with the occasional smack to his rump, increasing the hardness every now and again, as Garry kept on with his vocalisations. The slapping action made Marrilyn think of her lovely mount, Hot to Trot, who, when being trained for the Garryowen event, loved a bit of a slap on the rump and a stroke on his sweat-sheened neck, particularly following a big, collected canter of figure of eights in the manege arena.

He had been a big strong gelding who had sailed over jumps with a steady mind, and drifted about the dressage arena collected up and floating, as if he could walk on air. It had been a sad day when Frankcombe, the vet, had to put him down due to his age. Hot to Trot was buried under the giant oak, next to the bluestone stables, and every day as Marrilyn went about her business on the farm, directing the men, drifting mobs steadily across wintertime paddocks with her kelpie dogs, she missed him terribly.

Hot to Trot had been the love of her life, especially due to the fact that that bounder, Hugo, had left her, without so much as a 'toodle-pip'. It was not long after they'd lost the baby. Hot to Trot had filled the emotional void for a decade. Thank god the horse had then come into her life.

And now, thank god King had come along, she mused. She had got King as a puppy after Father had passed, as a gift from Father's elderly friend Angus McRodgers. Angus had an exclusive line of kelpies, the bloodlines of which were mostly kept under lock and key and not shared with the wider world beyond his farm. Since that time, King had certainly opened up her world. Through the Yard Dog Trial circuit, the kelpie had given her new experiences, new places and lovely people. *Very* lovely people, if today's joining was anything to go by, Marrilyn thought happily.

After only three seasons in working-dog sports, she was excelling. This year she had blitzed the trial season with King. The Australian working-dog world had been witness to this remarkable dog and his handler and their perfect synergy in moving sheep through the yards. On the farm, King was an all-rounder in his work abilities and had a very fine temperament. This year, since winning the national championship, requests came in for access to his bloodlines. Suddenly Marrilyn and King were being visited by the finest kelpie bitches from across Australia.

The vehicles would roll in along the pine-lined drive of Glencraig Estate and the dog men would tumble out, crumpled from travel, and then hitch bitches on leads and seek out her King. The men knew that the genetics contained within his glossy black-and-tan body were utterly special and rare and his first pups on the ground were showing true ability. She had hiked up her service fee to put some of the kelpie men off, but they just seemed to keep coming as word spread.

She looked at the dog tenderly now through the French doors to the deck where he was still knotted painfully to Cindy, the pink of his swollen penis angling awkwardly backwards from its sheath. There was a look of worry in his eyes that the excited bitch might suddenly move again and reef on his 'whatnot'. She noticed the saliva was dripping from King's long pink tongue as he swivelled and whined a little from the pain of being caught, knotted. He really needed a drink of water, she thought. King looked into Marrilyn's eyes through the glass panes, as if to say, 'I've done the fun bit of the job. How long will this next bit take?'

Dog joining always looked so rewarding for the dogs at the start, with all the tail wagging and play bouncing, but it could end so horribly at the finish for the male if the bitch was skittish. Poor King.

Marrilyn wondered how her own coupling with Garry would end too? She must remember to offer Garry water when they were done. Then she began to wonder when *would* he be done? Hugo had always been so quick at it. Hardly a bother, really. You barely had to put down your book. Not like Garry, who was clearly a bit of a stayer, especially considering his age. In fact, he could almost enter the Tom Quilty without a horse, he seemed that much of an endurance man, Marrilyn realised happily!

As Garry upped his pace and started thrusting like a barley-crushing machine and Marrilyn again felt the budding of her clitoris in response to the sexual stimulation, she was getting an idea why King got so excited when the farmers brought their kelpie females to him for joining. This was feeling rather good, Marrilyn thought, as she gave Garry another slap on his rather flaccid buttock. If she had a tail, she felt she'd certainly be wagging it now! She wanted to start panting too, like a bitch in heat, but she thought Garry might find that behaviour unseemly. Instead, she let a few vowel sounds go herself.

It was fortunate, given Garry's lengthy performance, that Marrilyn was a strong, fit woman for her age. As she now pushed her pelvis upwards against Garry, she decided she would aim to move her hips as if competing at Grand Prix Dressage. It had been several years since she had been on a horse, but one never forgot.

The tilting of her pelvis back and forth as if doing a fine piaffe had an instant effect on Garry.

'Oh, my lord,' he declared in a deep baritone.

As she lay beneath him, she decided to try a half-pass this way, and then again that way, falling into a perfect pattern and rhythm with her hip raisings. Just when she felt Garry was on the brink, she executed a quick flying change and slowed her pace. Then Marrilyn began to piaffe again with her hips from beneath. This, to her excitement, seemed to elicit a strong sensation in her own body and clearly had the desired effect on Garry. With some big piaffe movements that snaked her body up and down on the floor, she could soon hear Garry's home-straight heavy breathing in her ear as he galloped home. She joined him on the home-straight too, and as she sailed over a brush fence with a cry, she climaxed just as Garry ejaculated inside her. Delightedly she listened to Garry crying out as he belted past the winning post: 'Oh ma'am, oh ma'am! Yes! Yes!' as if the Queen had surprised him with a wonderful gift of a corgi or a Badminton horse, or some such thing.

As Garry lay on top of her, spent and puffing, Marrilyn patted his shoulder like he was her Hot to Trot. He had truly done a fine thing for her and she was well pleased, even grateful, for what had passed between her and this quiet, formal, kindly gent this afternoon.

'I think we have had a successful joining,' Marrilyn said, smiling, and Garry mumbled a happy agreement, his face still buried in the scoop of her neck.

Marrilyn had found this particular experience very invigorating indeed. In a kind of animalistic way. As if she had just ridden hard with the Hunt Club and scored a fox.

'Another cup of tea?' she asked, and Garry nodded acceptance.

A week later Marrilyn clipped King on the tray of the Glencraig work ute and climbed in to begin her routine morning drive to the sheds to give the workmen their instructions for the day. On the way she stopped at the big Glencraig letterbox, and was surprised by a parcel amongst the bills and rural papers.

As she undid the package, she discovered the most splendid-looking gift, wrapped in shiny, silken black paper tied with a wide, satin brown ribbon. Inside the box, carefully nestled in swathes of tissue paper, was the most beautiful fine bone china figurine of a kelpie, black and tan, just like King. There was also a note in a lovely rolling hand.

My Dearest Marrilyn,

Do come and stay! Might I suggest you bring King along too and together we can help Cindy whelp the pups. I believe they are due your birthday weekend in June.

Thank you so much for a very enjoyable visit. Here's an early birthday gift for your collection.

My fondest regards,

Garry Goodwood

P.S. 'Woof, Marrilyn darling, woof!'

Marrilyn smiled as she began to fold the letter and place the adorable figurine back in the safety of its box. Just then, her mobile rang.

'Hello. Mawwilyn Wuthbwidge speaking,' she said.

'Er. Hello. This is Humberston Peterson from Carnegie Downs. I've heard you offer services with your kelpie in your home?'

'This is twue! Indeed I do offer joinings,' Marrilyn said with a smile as she had the sudden realisation her life had just got very, very interesting. 'When would you like to come?'

Showtime
Line-up

*T*he green swathe of synthetic fake-grass carpet was illuminated vibrantly when Katie flicked the switches on the meter box. Suddenly the Royal Show's beef and dairy cattle pavilion was flooded with fluorescent white light, revealing Katie's band of five very merry, rum-soaked men who were running amok with her. For a moment she had to shield her eyes.

'Fark me!' said her friend Ben as he sank down on the first tier of one of the spectator stands and glanced around nervously. 'The security dude is gunna catch us for sure. Katie, I really think we oughta pack it in and go back to our swags. We could all get fired. Or arrested. Or ...'

'Grow a set,' Katie said as she thrust him a bottle of Bundy, 'and chill.'

Ben rolled his big dark eyes at her and adjusted the show ribbons that were slung about his neck. 'C'mon, Katie, it's nearly four. The sun will be up soon. You know you've got to get the cattle ...'

'Oh, shut up, Ben! You're such an old fuddy-duddy. Live a little,' she said, giving him a shove, then chuckling at the sight of him. Over Ben's broad farmer shoulders

153

were draped satin ribbons in royal blue, vibrant red and white, and some were printed with gold embossed writing and had yellow tassels fringing their ends. She plucked a rosette from his checked cowboy shirt and plopped it on his head. 'You look gorgeous, Priscilla Queen of the Show, so c'mon, don't be a wuss. Play with the rest of us,' she said as Ben looked at the toes of his R.M. Williams boots, a sullen expression on his face, while the other bleary-eyed fellas stood wobbly-booted around him.

The abundant ribbons with which Katie had dressed Ben were the result of today's city Royal Show judging and Katie's skill as a cattle handler. On Tuesday Katie would hand the ribbons and trophies to her boss, Ardlain Cattle Stud owner Mr Greenaway, when she returned to the property with the truckload of show cows and bulls. Old Mr Greenaway loved Katie and sent her around the country with his Herefords, from big inner-city shows to smaller country events. Thanks to her expert grooming, her no-bullshit-but-charming personality and ability to handle a beast in the showring, Ardlain was now attracting three times the going price for service fees and semen. Orders were so strong Mr Greenaway'd had to put another jackaroo on, a good-looking stupid one, much to Katie's delight. And Mr Greenaway had a burgeoning trophy cabinet. When it came to work and cattle, there was nothing slack about Katie.

She now ruffled Ben's hair. 'Sook,' she said, then with a determined look, fished around in her jeans pocket for a cigarette lighter. She turned to the boys and passed it to

Knackers, who stood centre of the group in his scuffed old Dogger boots and Irish rugby-union jumper. Next, Katie thrust an armful of show program newspapers at the tall, solid Skipper. 'There you are, Skip, sunshine. You're in charge of Tim and Knackers. You're on. Now go get ready. It's showtime!'

The boys grinned widely as if they had just been given the keys to a new V8 ute to play with.

'I'll be back,' said Knackers in a deep Arnie Schwarzenegger voice, thrusting out his chest and flexing out his farmboy arms. Katie laughed as she watched them disappear — Skip, Tiny Tim from Tamworth and Knackers — swaggering with drunkenness around the corner. Dave and Ben remained on the seating, watching them go and passing the Bundy bottle back and forth between each other, Katie noting that Ben did not take a swig every time. Dave, on the other hand, was getting more and more legless.

'This is gunna be good.' She grinned.

Katie was more sober than the boys, as was her way. On big nights like this on the cattle show circuit, Katie played along with the boys, but underneath, she was enjoying her own private kind of game.

Like the conductor of an orchestra, Katie had become a master at guiding the moves and mindsets of the drunken boys. It was kind of like a hobby. She would set up scenarios for them to get into, then sit back and laugh as it unfolded or — in the case of most nights — unravelled. She liked to watch. And she especially liked to watch country boys in boots as they made total wallies of themselves. It was gold.

On nights she was in the mood (and most nights she was), she'd pick the best bloke of her group of cattle show mates and bed him for a night. The next day, acting still as if they were just mates, she'd key the random best-bloke's number into her phone for the next time she came into that particular town with the cattle. Her phone was chockers with a few lovely larrikin fellas and a lot of adorable dickheads, kind of like a scorecard, and life for the moment as a young single woman and stud groom was good for her.

Katie had made a pact with herself to have a goal or two in life. It was during a bender on her twenty-first with her mate, Tina, a truck driver from Mildura, that they had decided it would be a great idea to set a target for Katie: her goal was to bed fifty blokes by the time she was thirty-one. She had ten years to do it, and she knew she'd reach the target easily. After her quota of fifty, she planned to settle down, maybe, and have a couple of kids to at least one of the fellas. She was in no hurry.

Tina had dreamed up only three rules for her to follow, which were:

Rule number one: Bedding the same boy twice didn't count. She could only score him once on the card.

Rule number two: Always practise safe sex and use a condom (because as Tina had pointed out, 'after fifty bonks with random blokes your fanny will be like Shrek's swamp — festy and green').

Rule number three: Don't (whatever you do) get attached, or you won't make target.

At first Katie had gone on a spree, clocking up five guys in three weeks, texting Tina with her bounty. And Tina began to record Katie's bonk numbers in the back of her trucking log book. Country pubs were the best source, Katie found. Easy pickings with all those blokes in their high-vis workwear, full as boots, and a lot of them not wanting to go home to their bored and bitchy wives.

'You can spot the high-vis boys easy in the dark,' Katie told Tina once.

'Reckon we should've set the target at a hundred,' said Tina, who seemed to live vicariously through Katie's exploits as, weighing in at over one hundred kilos, and with a serious eczema problem, she never got laid.

Katie knew most of her girlfriends just wanted one fella, and would spend their time preening and prepping to bag a boyfriend. She watched them at the shows looking with puppy-dog eyes at the blokes. Blokes who would end up leaving them for another girl, or treating the girls like crap. Katie believed one bloke was trouble. You could get yourself stuck. You could get yourself hurt. Plus, she reasoned, why settle on just one bloke when there was an entire all-you-can-eat man banquet out there? To dine widely and frequently on an extensive menu of male was better than starving in a loveless, bitter relationship that beat you about the head and heart and eventually killed you … wasn't it? That was what had happened to Katie's mum. And Katie was buggered if she was going to suffer the same fate.

She remembered sitting on the edge of her mother's bed, her mother's hair falling from her paper-thin scalp to drift around with the fur of the cat. At the time, Tigger could always be found curled in the crook of one of the bony angled limbs of her mother. The two of them dozing as both cat and human created tiny tumbleweeds of auburn and tabby hair that would eddy away across the bed on the breeze from the open window. Outside, Katie recalled seeing her father, stooped and swearing, jerking the resistant pull-start cord of the lawnmower. The grass was practically up to his knees.

Katie knew he was only mowing it because the neighbours had complained again and had threatened to dob him into the RSPCA about the flyblown sheep he kept on his one-acre block. He certainly wasn't cutting the grass to make a nicer view from the window for her mother. He wouldn't help move the heavy old metal bed and sagging mattress when Katie asked, so all her mother had been able to see were the oily old forty-four gallon drums lined up against the wall of the rusting, sagging shed. Most of the drums were overflowing with her dad's beer longnecks and her brother's empty cans of pre-mix grog. The other thing in view was the broken Hills Hoist that her youngest brother, Jade, had snapped when he swung on it one Christmas Day with Travis after they had snuck booze from the old man.

Katie sighed. One useless father and five drop-kick brothers — six men who couldn't keep the garden nice, or do a load of washing to save themselves. They didn't know where the kitchen sink was, let alone the dishwashing liquid. They only knew how to buy boxes of beer and seventy-five cent loaves of white bread, and how to leave toast crumbs scattered across the kitchen bench. Katie constantly came home from school to dirty dishes where baked beans had erupted and overflowed like lava down the sides of plastic bowls. The microwave too would be crusted with acidic crud, like toxic waste, and there were the lidless containers of melting margarine sitting in patches of sunlight, drooling into oil slicks. No one would fix the dripping tap, or change the toilet rolls, or scrub the mould from the shower bay that was skid-mark brown with artesian bore water anyway.

Her father was just as bad as the brothers and contributed to the piles of teetering dirty plates and the soup of foul language and aggression that washed through the house. Useless, thought Katie again. It had been down to her … just because she had a fanny. *All because she had a fanny.* As far as she could figure, the boys got out of it because they had dicks. Where was the sense and logic in this world? Katie couldn't reckon it.

She could see her dad from where she sat on her mum's bed. The red flush of his wide frustrated caveman forehead, his giant belly rounding out in front of him. As he stooped over the mower again, adjusting the choke, Katie wanted to take a tyre wrench to the back of his head. She felt her jaw clench. Her mum's big haunted gaze had slid across to where Katie was looking, her eyes blinking slowly and her pale tongue dragging hopelessly over parched lips.

'Arsehole,' her mum had said. 'He'll never win. He can't get me now.' She plucked at the chenille bedspread with a clawlike hand.

But Katie knew he already had won. He had got her mother. And soon, Katie knew, she would be alone.

Before her mum died, she had told Katie to 'live life to the full'. Several times. 'Don't make the same mistakes I did, girl.'

She made Katie promise that she would. At the time, Katie wasn't sure what 'living life to the full' meant. After the funeral, when Katie had cleared out for good, hitching with just one bag on the roasting highway north, she had pondered the concept often. 'Live life to the full.' How did you do that?

Surely it meant not marrying a dirty down-and-out loser who would beat his wife and children and would hire hookers on trucking runs?

So, Katie's target of fifty men and her complete freedom remained. Her job as a well-travelled stud groom meant life was full and interesting. She smiled beneath the bright spotlights of the pavilion and glanced over to Dave and Ben and wondered wickedly which stud she'd choose to groom tonight.

Ben was out. He was a sulker and a bit of a poof. Not as in gay, but as in that soft-cock, sensitive kind of way. When she saw him at the shows, he would rush up to give her big bear hugs and tell her she was beautiful. He would bounce around her like a happy dog wagging not just its tail, but its whole body, and when Ben was done gushing with 'It's great to see you again, Katie!' he'd hang around her like a bad smell. Plus, he was always trying to have deep and meaningful chats — a 'D&M', as he put it — with her about how she was feeling after her 'mum's passing'. Ben's mum had croaked a few years back too, so he kept trying to tell her they had a lot in common. Ben was always saying he wanted to spend time with her, so they could help each other through. Help her through *what*? Katie had wondered. She was out of that house. Her mum was dead and buried. She was through.

And what did they have in common? Everyone's mother died, eventually. He was the lucky one. Nothing for *him* to work through. He was the son of a big-time cattle farmer who had everything, whereas she came from nothing and had nothing. Plus, he was always trying to persuade her to go out to dinner or the movies with him, 'like a proper girl on a proper date', and she knew, even though he never said it, he didn't like this whole fifty men thing she and Tina had dreamed up. When she talked about it, he went quiet. Then he'd softly ask her again to come out to his beef property, 'to see his cows' and for some 'time out'. Time out from what? Katie wondered. From living life to the full? He really gave her the shits. Ben was very good-looking in that chunky beef farmer kind of way, but his behaviour towards her was just plain weird. Best to steer clear of him, she thought tonight, as she stood in the cattle show pavilion.

She turned her attention to Dave. He was a redhead so he wasn't an option. Nice though he was, she'd always questioned the temperaments of redheads ... a legacy of her father's rude and arrogant red kelpie, aptly but unimaginatively named Red. The dog had bitten her suddenly and sharply on her hand once when she'd reached up to climb into the cab of her dad's truck. So if Ben and Dave were out, that left the other three.

At that moment, as if on cue, and as Katie had suggested to them, the rest of the mob, Tim, Skip and Knackers, came flaring into the showring, rolled newspapers set alight and jammed in their butt-cracks. They sprinted with flames and smoke streaming from their arse cheeks, not a stitch on, save for their boots. They did a couple of victory laps, arms held upwards to the high metal beams of the giant empty shed, Bundy cans clutched in their hands, penises flipping from side to side as they ran, tails ablaze. The newspaper ash drifted down to the carpet of green where only a few hours earlier dairy cows with giant udders had paraded slowly by like a fleet of ships emerging from the doldrums. How different was this parade, Katie thought gleefully, as she watched the naked idiots flying around the arena.

'Flaming arseholes!' chorused Tiny Tim from Tamworth and Big Skip as they lapped the showring. Knackers followed with a call of 'Great balls of fire!'. The whooping rose up to the rafters and startled the sleeping sparrows. Some of the tiny birds fluttered about, confused by the smoke, the bright lights and the noise, then the birds again settled on the rafters, their feathers ruffled. Below, the paper extinguished in fine blackened drifts and the boys fell about laughing, still lit up with excitement, the smell of smoke permeating the large building. Katie clapped and whooped from the stand as did Dave and Ben, smiles cast broadly on their faces.

'Gold!' Katie said. 'Pure gold!'

She watched as the boys tackled each other and fell about like a pile of rollicking puppies, wrestling wildly, straining, young healthy limbs tangled. They grunted with effort, their chests rising and falling with hysterical laughter. Katie glimpsed their tackle on the flop between their legs, as they rumbled and hauled against each other. She liked the look of the muscular thighs of Tim, short though his legs were, and the way the blond hair on his chest looked soft to touch. Skip had a nice, high, rounded arse, which would be good to grab in the missionary position pump, thought Katie. And as for Knackers, well … if he was anything to go by on the slack, he'd be a good bull when he was on the full. He had a massive dong!

It was too hard to choose with them all raucous and tumbling like that. Katie decided to instil some order. She stood abruptly, took the show ribbons that hung from Ben's shoulders and strode out into the showring, shouting, 'Ladies and gentlemen, boys and girls! It is now time for our most prestigious event. Drumroll, please, Dave …' She swept her arm in Dave's direction, who thrummed his boots on the steel flooring of the spectator stands. 'I give you the Supreme Champion Boy of the Show!'

The boys looked up at her from where they panted, still lying in their nude-style world wrestling pile. They took in Katie's stance, looking for all the world like Wonder Woman out to get a bit. Her broad shoulders, tapering to a cinched-in waist, the long curving line of her strong, muscled legs in tight skinny jeans that ran to her Dogger work boots, her shining, glossy dark hair falling over her shoulders and a nice set of dairy pillows that held themselves out like a full spinnaker sail in front of her. It was Katie's tits that held the boys' eyes and their imaginations. The boys, who saw Katie from time to time on the show circuit, all talked about Katie's norks when she wasn't in earshot to punch them. They surmised how they might swing and sway and jiggle when she was on the buck. The boys often talked of Katie and fantasised about her. They all loved Katie. She was a good chick-bloke. A good mate, and bloody funny. And when they had their beer-goggles on, she was hot and a girl they would 'do'. But most of the time she was one of them. Part of the crew. She was always up for any kind of fun. And here she was, at it again.

'Hands and knees, boys. Now! In a line,' she commanded. The boys, up for the laugh, obeyed her.

'Hold on!' Dave shouted from the stand. He suddenly stood and began to tear off his clothes. 'Wait for me!'

The other boys whooped and hollered when Dave revealed lily-white skin that was fuzzed with red hair from his chest to his toes. He cupped his hands over his privates and grinned as he tiptoed over to the pile of naked men.

'What? So what if it's red?' he said, looking down, frowning at his own body. He shrugged. 'At least my mother loves me, no matter what.'

'Only a mother could! Didn't know rangas could enter,' Skip said.

'Git out of it, you red beast,' Tim said. 'This judging class is only for us Angus studs. Not a throwback ginger minge like you. You can't be in the line-up!'

Ignoring him, Dave eagerly joined them on all fours.

Skip eyed Dave's tufts of curling ginger pubic hair. 'Why hello, fanta pants!'

'Shut the fuck up, Skipper,' Dave said.

Skip gave him a shove and for a moment the wrestle was on until Katie's loud whistle pierced the air.

'Enough, bulls! Line-up, now!'

The boys settled and quietened. Dave spluttered laughter at the situation he found himself in. Knackers grinned like a village idiot. From the stands, Ben looked skywards to the rafters, rolled his eyes and blew out a tired breath.

'We are so gunna get sprung!' he said.

'Hey, Benno,' called Tim. 'You joining us?'

'Yes, Ben,' Katie said, turning to him. 'Are you entering the Supreme Champion Boy of the Show? There's a trophy for the champ.'

'Me? Nah, mate, count me out.'

'Suit yourself,' she said, then turned back to the other boys. As she looked at them naked before her, lined up on all fours, she felt a shiver of power ripple through her body and a rush of desire that made her nipples sting ever so slightly.

Suddenly her one-of-the-boys demeanour altered altogether. Her voice deepened provocatively. 'I've decided, on seeing you studs before me, that the trophy tonight … will be me.' She pointed to herself. 'For one night only. Anything you want me to do, I'll do. If you want to "do" me, I'll do you.'

The boys' mood instantly shifted. Desire flared in some of their eyes. Others swallowed nervously at the prospect.

Ben glanced at her, his face pale, his dark eyes uncertain. He grabbed up the bottle and stalked out of the pavilion.

'Where're you going?' she demanded, her eyes narrowing.

He didn't answer. She brushed the thought away that he was angry with her and turned her attention back to the boys.

'Everyone else in? Who would like Miss Katie as a prize?'

All of them nodded gleefully. Katie smiled at her control. Earlier today, when she stood in the judging line-up with the washed and glossed Ardlain Hereford cattle, she had conjured up this scenario in her mind. Right from when the last ribbon was draped across the wide shoulders of Supreme Champion Bull of the Show, Katie had been on a mission to get the boys to where they were right now ... in the showring, naked, for her to play with.

Katie, who had been involved in junior judging of livestock with her high school group since she was thirteen, was no stranger to the process of judging beasts. It was easy to play-act this role. She stood alongside Tim, beginning at his head.

'Now, let's take a look at this stud. What have we here?' She placed her fingertips on his crown and ran her fingers firmly over his scalp, stooping over him, making sure his eyes could not miss the deep, tanned line of cleavage framed by her tight-fitting red R.B. Sellars work shirt, undone very low. She ran her finger over his lips lightly and grabbing his jaw, opened his mouth. She nodded and smiled.

'Good, nice teeth. Good-looking head.' Then she ran her hands over his scalp again. 'Glossy, healthy coat. Good muscling on the neck and shoulders,' she said, her touch drifting lower. 'Nice back line, but what about the legs and the business end? Would you make the stud herd? Are you leggy enough to get up on a girl?' Her dominatrix tone of voice, and her touch on his skin, flowed through Tim's body and hit his cock. As she ran her fingertips firmly down the muscles of his back, he remained on all fours, but she could see goosebumps travelling over his white skin.

By the time her hands roved over his buttocks his cock was raging hard, the head of it almost touching his flat stomach as it flexed in excitement. It was small, but neat, as far as penises went. She noticed the other boys were starting to harden up. She felt a gush of wetness between her legs. Could she do it? Could she take them all on? Or should she not pig out on this smorgasbord lined up before her ... should she just choose the one? Could she stop at just one?

'I see you're ready for joining,' she said to Tim. 'I like that in a stud.' She lightly slapped him on the arse and walked over to Skip.

Katie began the same process. She liked the feel of Skip's soft, blond-brown hair, the way his golden skin ran over his taut muscles. His job as a fencing contractor showed through on his body: his arm muscles rolled beautifully under his skin down to his strong tanned hands, where his long fingers were splayed on the fake-grass carpet, and he had lovely broad shoulders. The weight of him would feel good beneath her. She ran her hand over his back, pressing her fingertips into his flesh as if fat-scoring a prime lamb.

'Oh, that is one nice bit of beef,' she said. She slapped him hard on the buttock, then she left him suddenly and moved to inspect Knackers.

'Hey!' protested Skip. 'Aren't you going to check my nuts, baby? I could be a better stud than those guys for you.'

'Quiet, you!' she said commandingly. Another flush of wanting came deep within her. She could barely believe her luck — or, rather, her cleverness at creating this scene before her. All these boys, aroused and ready for her. She couldn't wait. She was raging with horniness. She wanted to take them all. But should she? Something outside herself seemed to be trying to reach her. Annoyed by the invasion in her mind, she tried to focus on the moment.

She moved to Knackers, where she smoothed a palm over Knackers's freckled back and noticed the hairs tufting on his shoulders. That ruled him out. She liked a cleanskin man on the shoulders. She gave a cursory glance at Dave, ruffling his red hair.

'You are a genetic freak even though I love you, but sorry, Dave, you're end of the line.'

'Aw!' Dave protested.

'I've made my decision,' she said as she began to drape the ribbons across the backs of the boys, finishing with Skip as the Supreme Champion Boy of the Show. She laid the thick tricoloured sash across his wide, perfect shoulders, then swung a leg over his back and sat astride him.

'Giddy up, cowboy,' she said. 'You are the winner. What is it you want me to do for you?'

Skip rolled over on his back, desire in his eyes, Katie still straddling him, his cock nudging at the seams of her jeans where her ready pussy waited hungrily. The other boys crowded around, filled with intrigue and lust as they watched Katie begin to French kiss Skip slowly.

Suddenly a loud, deep voice shouted into the echoing void of the show pavilion. 'Oi! Security! Stay right there!'

Pandemonium ensued. The boys instantly scattered, most of them forgetting their pile of clothing by the stands, just bolting, naked, for the shadows. Skip pushed Katie off him and ran. Katie was left there, sprawled on the ground in stunned surprise. She watched as Dave picked up his clothes and raced for the big door, slipping out with a rattle of tin.

Katie stood up and looked to where the voice had come from, a look of worry crossing her face. But then, she reasoned, the voice of the security guard had been male. She could play this one. She decided she'd check him out before she ran. Adrenaline coursed through her system and excitement roamed across her face. She could get into trouble … but Katie loved trouble. She waited for the guard to come, but nothing happened

'Hello?' she said, her voice echoing in the giant empty pavilion.

There was a loud clank and the building was suddenly consumed by darkness. The show was over.

She swallowed nervously. This was not how she'd planned it. Katie was about to run, but she couldn't see a thing. It was pitch black. She spun about when she heard a noise behind her.

'Hello,' she said, the nervousness quavering her voice a little. 'This is creeping me out. Who's there?'

She remained in the middle of the showring and felt fear grab her.

Suddenly a torch flicked on. The light in her face was blinding. She held her hand up to reduce the glare.

'Just what do you think you are doing?' came the stern voice. 'This is show property! You should be ashamed of yourself.'

'Hang on a minute,' Katie said, a quizzical smile lighting her face. 'Ben? Is that you?'

No answer. The torch came nearer.

'Stop it,' Katie said, putting an arm up to her face and turning her head away. 'You're blinding me.'

'Shut up. You're under arrest.'

'It is you, Ben. Isn't it? You sly and dirty dog! You scared the crap out —'

'Quiet!' he shouted. His voice in the darkness was harsh. Angry, even. 'I said, you are under arrest.'

She laughed nervously. He sounded really upset. Really angry.

'What for, Ben?'

The light was turned away slightly as his voice softened. 'For getting so lost in life that you think it's okay to gangbang a bunch of blokes.'

'That's it?' Katie was seeing red now. 'Fuck off, Ben. What I do is my business.'

'No, I won't fuck off! Oh, Katie, I wish you would wake up. I wish you could see you are so cut up about your mum dying that you are one angry bird and you hate your dad so much that you have no room to love yourself.'

'Fuck off, Ben,' she said angrily to the darkness, 'I can do what I like. I'm not lost in life, you tosser. I'm living life to the full. And you just ruined my night.'

'Ruined it? You're causing chaos, Katie! Living life to the full is letting yourself be loved. Not slutting about with so much denial that you can't see you're treating yourself poorly. And treating blokes like shit, not to mention the wives and girlfriends you've inadvertently hurt. You need self-love, Katie, not fifty fucks.'

'Bugger off, Mr Dalai fucking Lama. I get plenty of love,' Katie said. 'Go away, Ben, and leave me alone. Loser.'

'Katie,' he said softly, 'I've been watching you. For a year now. It has got to stop. You think you're having fun. But what is really going on? Huh? How do you really feel the next day? How do you really feel? Afterwards.'

'I can do whatever the fuck I want. And why should you care!' she shouted then, turning her back to where his voice was coming from, every muscle in her body tense. Emotion buried far below bubbled up from an unknown place. She could feel Ben in the darkness. Not his body, but his energy. She recalled all the times he'd hovered near when she'd shagged some other guy. It was he who had brought her coffee in the morning in the cattle stalls, and bacon and egg rolls when she was hungover, and made her laugh when she felt like crying. It was he who called her on a Wednesday night, after memories of the weekend adventures with other men had turned cold in Katie's heart. It was Ben, Katie thought. Ben. He was the Supreme Champion. A Champion of Kindness. Tears spilled down her cheeks. Angrily she swiped them away.

'How dare you,' she said.

She heard the torch switch off and she was left in the pitch black. Next she felt a hand reach out for hers. His touch was gentle. Coaxing. And then his arms were about her from behind. She felt the warmth and solidity of his big body press against her back. Softly Ben shivered the palms of his hands up and over the skin of her arms. She felt as if an angel had touched her. She sighed a long breath that seemed to soften her whole being.

In the darkness, his gentle touch turned her about to face him. She could hear his breath, feel him millimetres away from her. She felt his full lips press gently onto hers, his fingers reach up to brush over her face, through her long hair, and she felt sparks, like stars shooting across the blackness of her mind. Her knees trembled and her breath was suddenly fluttering lightly, like the wings of birds. They pressed their bodies closer together and French kissed slowly. The tenderness of him was mesmerising. When their lips drew apart, she felt as if she had swum in a timeless, dreamlike universe of kissing.

'How could you want me?' she said, her cheeks wet from tears she hadn't even felt herself cry.

Ben guided her hand down to the front of his jeans where his firmness was waiting for her. 'I want you, Katie. Not for one night. For more than that. You deserve more.'

She felt her body give way in a sob. He held her for a time, the sadness washing through her in waves, overlaid with even more waves of desire. She began to kiss him back with more conviction. With an instinct that she had no way of stopping.

He peeled away her shirt and bra. She felt the delicious scratch of the coarse carpet on her back as he lay her out in the darkness. She felt his warm wet mouth on her erect nipples and his big hands scooping up her giant melon-shaped breasts. He sparked kisses down her stomach, over her rounded belly, and next he was gently unbuckling her rodeo belt and tugging her jeans down. There she felt his lips suck and his tongue flutter over her ripened clit. She ran her fingers through his soft hair and arched her back. He thrust a finger in and, with love and the thrusting of his perfectly timed fingers, Katie rose up to the stars in the finest, most intensely felt of slow dreamy orgasms … she was lost in that otherworldly place. No longer counting numbers. No longer scoring victories. No longer adrift and alone in life. No longer fighting. When she returned from that place in the galaxy, Ben came to lie on top of her and kissed her slowly along the smooth skin of her neck. She put her arms around him and pulled his weight down onto her. He felt so solid. So real.

'I want you, Katie. You.' He pulled away and she heard the tearing of a foil wrapper, the unzipping of his jeans and then, deliciously, she felt his raging hardness as he slid deeply into her and moaned her name.

He said it as if her name was the most special thing in the world.

She had never heard her name said this way. She shut her eyes and hoped that this was the end and the beginning all at the same time.

She felt his breath on her neck as he pushed into her, and then, with a lover deep within her, Katie let herself go for the first time in her life. There in the darkness she allowed herself to be filled with one man's love. Letting him into her life.

In her voice, out loud, she heard herself say, 'You are number twenty-five. And you are pretty special.'

And as Ben slowly moved with her in the darkness, Katie realised she was halfway to fifty, but she knew it was time to stop, so that her life could truly begin.

Milking Time

*M*ary Milthorpe could tell cow Number 50 was in season by the way she was bulling her paddock mate. The cow was rearing up on her hocks and grappling the angled hips of young Dolly, who skittered forward with surprise at the sudden show of lust.

'Enjoy it, darlin',' Mary said as she grabbed the plastic yellow handpiece to disconnect the electric fence and open the single strand wire gate. 'Sadly, no real bulls round here. Only artificial insemination for you girls.'

Most of the Holstein herd were already waiting at the gate for milking. Mary was a little late this afternoon after having to put the Sunday roast on for tonight's tea.

'Okay, girls. I'm here now,' she said as she admired them in the sunlight. They were a good line, this lot. Big-framed girls with nicely set udders, wide-angled hips and deep, dark eyes speaking of docility and kindness … most of the time. When the hormones were running high, they got a bit stirry with each other. Occasionally the bossier ones needed to be kept in order by Sparky, but these days the poor old dog had completely lost his spark. Nowadays, Mary had to rely on a black length of poly pipe and a growl in her voice to get the cows unstuck from their arguing and flowing again along the lanes.

But even though Sparky was past his use-by date, she still took him with her just to keep the old dog happy. Mary sent Sparky out round the cows with a light whistle that she knew he could barely hear any more. He took off at an arthritic trot over the eaten-off pasture that was dotted with dollops of dung. She watched as the poor decrepit dog made a show of rousing the cows into one herd using his still-keen scent more than his foggy eyes. Mary sighed at the sight of him and of the kind cows playing along with the pretence, as if they too felt sorry for the old dog. He had been such a bright young pup and handsome too, in that red kelpie way.

Not these days though. Now his front paws were bent and twisted with arthritis and his coat was frizzled at the ends in a coarse fuzz. To add insult to the old fella, a few years back Sparky'd had the snip after getting the neighbour's bitch in pup one too many times. The same year that Maurice had his prostate worries.

'Gawd, Sparks,' Maurice had said, when first back from the doctor, and the dog fresh from the vet. 'You've come home two stone lighter in the back end and I've come home feeling like I've gone from being the bull around here to a useless old steer.' Then Maurice had taken his place on the verandah, gingerly settling in a deck chair, while Sparky splayed out with a sigh at Maurice's socked feet to begin the lengthy process of licking the wound where his balls used to be. Mary took on the milking by herself that day.

Milking Time

Mary grimaced when she thought of her memories of that time. Poor Maurice. Poor her! Dairy farming was hard enough on romance, let alone when Mary took into consideration her husband's inability these days to get it up.

She sighed as the black and white pond of milkers drained themselves from the paddock into the lane-way in their orderly cow way. As Mary saw cow Number 50 rise up again in a frisky show of 'mate your mate', she hoped that, back at the dairy, Maurice had enough shots of semen in the canister to cover all the girls who were cycling. It was like him to run out of the stuff.

The thought of semen prompted another meandering train of internal dialogue as Mary followed the cows along the lane. How long had it been since she'd got any action? She suddenly realised she'd been hitting the side of her gumboot hard with the poly, making a hollow plastic thwacking noise against her leg, which was hastening the cows. She stopped the unconscious action as the answer came to her. It must be at least twelve months. No wonder she was frustrated. Their lack of bedroom mojo hadn't really bothered her until recently. God knows they were dairy farmers and she was a woman, so she had, for the most part, been too buggered for any kind of hanky-panky over the years.

There was the milking to be done twice daily: morning and night. Then there was both calf and child rearing. And the housework.

No wonder she was too tired to even think about a bonk. But lately, like a calm sea about to be turmoiled by storms, Mary had been feeling a swell moving deep within her. A slow, aching longing. It hadn't helped that she'd been reading some of that 'nanna porn' that had been getting about in the supermarket. She'd recently picked up a copy of the book everyone was talking about. A bargain at twelve bucks. She'd spotted it as she'd mindlessly ambled down aisle five. It was sitting between the battery section and the magazines. She could do with some literature, she thought to herself, as she popped a copy into the trolley next to her supply of teabags and toilet rolls. All the ladies at craft were talking about it. Quite disturbing. But, she reasoned, when in Rome, or in her case, Ringarooma … better get up with the trend.

At first, it was difficult to stay awake reading the book due to exhaustion after her busy days. And then there was Maurice. He complained about the bedside light being on for too long. But, after a week or more, she'd read to chapter seven. By that stage she didn't know what the fuss was about, but, nonetheless, her nocturnal reading had caused her to lie awake listening to Maurice snoring and had switched her brain onto a treadmill. Each night she had wondered if she might be brave enough to walk her hand beneath the sheets over to the sleeping Maurice and begin to stroke his thighs and even further … higher up. She didn't want to push him. He was already closed off and touchy on the subject of his old fella. Instead, Mary would roll over, thrust her pillow under her head and lie in a state of restlessness and dozing non-sleep, knowing that soon the alarm would shrill in the darkness and it would be time to milk the girls.

As she trudged behind the cows, she thought about her Maurice and what he had been as a young man. And what he'd become. And together, what they had evolved to be as man and wife. Thirty years of milking the cows twice a day with him. Six hundred cows. Two hundred and fifty acres of irrigation. Three kids grown and gone. Bitterly cold winters with frosts and daily cattle feedings of hay. Stinking hot summers with flies and cowpats baked warm and moist beneath a sun-crusted top. Along with a dairy effluent pond that seemed to cast a shadow of stink over her house and the neglected, tufted garden.

Poor Maurice. Poor her. No wonder things were flaccid between them. But they did love their cows. And she knew, deep down, they did love each other in a real-life kind of way. Not like the people in the book.

Maybe, Mary thought, today was a day to make a change. Perhaps she and Maurice ought to go to the pub for a counter meal … or even grab a six-pack of beer and go for a dip in the dam. They hadn't done that in *years*. It was summertime, after all, and didn't most folk do something other than work in the summer? Mary looked about at the vibrant green pasture that had been blissfully heated by the hot day. She could feel the afternoon sun wrap warmly around the back of her neck, like a tender hand was resting there. As she soaked up the feeling, she pictured Maurice. His hands on her large breasts. In her mind's eye, she blocked out the image of his beer belly and bald head, and focused on his strong dairyman's arms and broad shoulders. If she squinted when she pictured him and put him in a hat, he was still a bit of alright for his age. Yep, if she squinted, there was still something about that man. She let out a breath. It was a relief to know she still felt something for him, after all these years. Yes, she resolved, it was definitely time to do something different. And today was the day.

She hastened the pace of the cows along the lane, the ones at the back casting her the occasional mildly dirty look. As they made their way, Mary watched their flicking tails and the swing of their low udders, and the compression of their hocks as they trod the well-worn track. Number 50 was still bulling. It was nice someone had the urge, Mary mused to herself. They were almost to the dairy and she thought of the task to be done tonight after milking, artificially inseminating the cows in oestrus. It would take the best part of an hour. Sorting the girls who were in season, drafting them off, separately putting each one into the crush. Maurice donning the glove, she smearing it with lube, he pushing his hand gently into the anus of cow Number 50, uttering soothing tones. Mary passing him the silver sliver of an AI gun freshly filled from the canister. The dry-ice mist drifting up in the still summer air. She liked the thought of the new calves on the ground, but getting the cows up the duff was so time consuming … it made the day long. She wondered if her oven roast would go dry back in the kitchen. She hoped she had it turned on low enough. She sighed again with a kind of longing. She thought of Maurice's prostate and the scare it had given him. She thought of that book. She thought of the AI lube that she had just bought. Then suddenly Mary Milthorpe knew exactly what she had to do.

In the yard, Mary swung the steel gate behind the last of the girls. Instead of hunting them up into the dairy, like she normally did, she walked purposefully around the back of the dairy to the workroom. She smiled. From the box on the shelf she pulled out two plastic elbow-length gloves. Then she grabbed up the two-litre pump pack of lube and marched round to the pit where Maurice was reaching for his milker's apron.

'You haven't let 'em up yet?' he said, barely glancing at her, his thick eyebrows raised enquiringly at her.

'No,' she said. She didn't move.

After a time he looked at her fully and his face clouded with more puzzlement when he saw her holding the gloves and lube.

'What? What are you doing? We'll do the inseminating after the milking. Yeah?' She could tell from the way he said it, Maurice was thinking she had clean gone off her rocker and maybe she was getting that old timer's disease.

She narrowed her eyes and walked directly to him. She stood before him. 'I want you,' she said.

'Huh! For what? Is there a cow down?' Maurice cocked his head when he asked and continued to throw the heavy milking apron over his head. Mary stopped him. She grabbed the apron, removed it from his grasp and returned it to the hook.

'Got one in season,' she said, her head tilted to one side as if to be alluring and raised her eyebrows up and down, so they danced like worms on strings.

Maurice frowned and shook his head. 'We'll deal with her later.' She could tell Maurice was annoyed now. He was reaching again for the apron. 'Like I said, we'll do the AI-ing after the milking.'

'We'll deal with her *now*,' Mary said. The way she spoke pulled Maurice up short. He hadn't heard that tone in his wife's voice for years. He hung the apron back on the hook and turned to her, an expression of enquiry on his face.

Mary sucked in a breath. Her large bosom rose upwards like a raft inflating. In the book, the woman had always looked up at the man through her long eyelashes. She tried it on Maurice now.

'You right?' he said. 'Got something in your eye?'

'No,' she said.

Suddenly she realised she had to be quite bossy — like the man had been with the girl in the book. She sniffed and lifted her chin in a determined way. 'I want you,' she said hoarsely.

'For what?'

'For this …' She reached up and kissed him square on the lips. His hands grasped her shoulders and he held her away a little.

'Mary. Later. After the milking,' Maurice said, a furrow on his brow, his eyes sliding away in shame.

'No. Now,' she said gently.

'What's the point …'

She raised a finger to his lips. 'Shush. Come.'

Mary took Maurice by the hand and led him around the back of the dairy, calling, 'Stay!' to old Sparky, who, with his fogged-up eyes, crabbed his way to lie in the shade of the ute.

They walked the short distance to paddock five, which cast itself out from the dairy in a swathe of lush meadow. The rounded leaves of clover and glossy stems of grasses rose up richly, ready for Wednesday's grazing. As Mary dropped her husband's hand to unhitch the gate chain, she glanced at him. There was a frown on Maurice's face. A confusion. But also, Mary noticed, there was an edge of excitement. A glint in his eyes. His breath had quickened. He was going along with her so far.

She allowed him to pass, then she set down the lube and gloves and shut the gate, dropping the metal loop over the lug, the metal head of which reminded Mary of the smooth crown of Maurice's thickened penis. She felt a shiver of anticipation. She turned to him, letting the heat of the earth rise up through the soles of her gumboots. She kicked them off, peeled her socks from her feet and sighed as she stepped onto the coolness of the grass.

'Well,' Maurice said, 'where's this girl in season?' He scanned the paddock, at last playing along with her.

'I'm right here,' Mary said and stepped forward before him.

Slowly she began to unbutton his shirt and draw it from him, the sun gleaming from the white skin of his belly, yet soaking into the deep brown of his arms. His curled, greying chest hair caught the light in a gingery-brown shine. Mary ran her fingers through it and leaned her head on his chest. She felt the warmth of him and his quickening of desire. Slowly, just like it had said in the book, Mary began to kiss and bite his neck, moving her lips down and running her tongue over his hair and skin to circle her tongue around his nipples. Mary watched as the tiny orbs came to life, like tiny, pink islands jutting from a smooth sea of skin. Suddenly hungry for him, she picked up the gloves and thrust them at him.

'Put these on,' she begged. Maurice looked at her, again confused, and was about to speak, but she continued: 'Shush. Put them on.'

His face was serious now. Not with a husband's expression of disdain or weariness, but an expression of want. For her. For sex. Maurice obeyed her, quickly dragging the gloves up his thick arms the way he had done so many times in the crush as he readied the girls for a dose of Holstein semen.

'Hold your hand out,' she said.

Maurice cupped his gloved fingers and Mary pumped a good blob of gel onto them.

'Shut your eyes.' Then she wrapped her hand around each of Maurice's fingers and she began to slowly pull up and down. Massaging his palms, sensually gliding pressure over each finger. The plastic and the lube slowly pistoning like a condom sheath on a cock with every stroke of her hand. Maurice let out a long breath from the sensation and she heard him give a little moan. She hoped the gesture she was performing on his fingers would be rushing blood to his cock. She looked down. Mary saw the bulge in his pants.

'Now take those off.' Mary nodded at his trousers.

Milking Time

Maurice's blue eyes flashed open and locked onto hers as he tugged at his belt and let his green KingGees fall to his ankles where they gathered at his boots. His breath was fast now, his chest rising and falling in the evening sunshine. She could see his erection bulging behind his navy supermarket Bonds. Mary set the lube down in the dense forest of clover, rye and phalaris. It was a good paddock, number five. The perfect choice, she thought.

Standing before him, she began to unbutton her faded navy drill shirt until her breasts billowed out white in the sun, as large as full balloons. Reaching round behind herself, she unhooked the thick strap of her bra and let it fall to the ground. The sight of her exposed breasts caused Maurice to tug his undies down a little, his gloved hands roaming up and over the shaft of his thick stub.

Mary stooped and squirted a huge dollop of lube into the palms of her hands and began to smear the gel over her breasts so her nipples stood out like two dark cherries. The lube was cold and clear like ice and the delightful shock of it on her skin made her gasp. Their eyes fixed together, Mary lay back in the grass, looking up at Maurice's cock emerging from his open shirt like a bayonet ready to charge. Mary began to unbutton her work jeans and writhe out of them. When Maurice saw the thick black hair of her bush, he fell to his knees before her, his cock pointing at her, pink and quivering in the sun. Hastily he pumped more lube into the palm of his hand and cupped it onto her sex. The ice-cold sting of it made Mary arch her back. Beneath the weight of her body she felt the lush clovers and grass stems explode juices and spread with each heavy press of her shoulder blades. The pungent smell of summer was smeared in green on her skin.

Maurice's fingers slid easily inside her and she groaned. First one, then two, then three, his hands and fingers working up and over her clitoris and into her vagina. The glove sliding too beneath the pressure of Maurice's fingers and the taut muscles of her enlivened sex.

His other gloved hand massaged soft gel over the snow-white skin of her jelly-like belly and breasts. Strong dairyman's hands probing and palpitating her ample womanly flesh. Grasping and releasing. Her giant udders swaying about from the quickness of her breath and Maurice's insistent touch. His hand slid further between her legs and she felt his fingers stroke the puckered skin of her arse. A fingertip ventured in and she groaned from the surprise of the feeling. The delight of it. Clear lube in every crevice and orifice. His condomed fingers sliding in and out of every place he could find. The weight of his body pressing alongside her, his cock's head jutting against her thigh, desperately waiting for its turn.

Maurice hastened his movement, pumping his fingers in and out of her, gliding over her clit. As she gave way to orgasm, her mouth opening up widely to the sky, Mary moaned so loudly the cows answered her from the dairy. Their deep, throaty lowing sent out moist vibrations of sound from across the electric fence. Mary orgasmed in waves against Maurice's strong fingers, her mouth still cast open in a now-silent cry with the dense damp grass pressing against her bare back.

Milking Time

Seeing his wife so, Maurice was in a frenzy now. She could see a solitary drop of clear liquid balancing on the slit eye of his cock. She cupped her giant double-D breasts together and invited Maurice's cock between the long line of her cleavage. He hastily drew off his boots and work trousers so he could straddle her. Sitting astride her tubby body, he plunged his cock into the tunnel of her breasts and began to move. There was so much lube, so much heat, that Mary thought her skin would burn red from the fire they were making of flesh pumping flesh under the sinking sun. Maurice's cock and the skin of her breasts made little squelching sounds like gumboots through mud, as she looked at his strong arms holding his body above her. She pressed her breasts closer together as Maurice began to pump a steady rhythm like the sucking cups on a milking machine. He was lost in what he was doing. His eyes shut. Sweat beading on his brow. Pump, suck, pump, suck. Mary arched her back and urged him on.

'Come on, baby! Come all over me.'

He responded by tit-fucking her harder. He thrust and thrust until suddenly the cows came home. Milky white sprayed upwards onto his wife's throat, then spilled onto the lush green clover, sweet enough to eat. Maurice, spent and panting, sweating and trembling, fell on her and lay there. She put her arms around him and kissed along his shoulders that were tufted with the same fine ginger hair of his chest.

When he got his breath back, Maurice rolled off her. Together they lay on their backs side by side dozing,

189

listening to the buzz of flies being carried on a gentle breeze far above the cowpats. A few straggling magpies called out in the dappled shade of the gums over by the house. Maurice slowly peeled one glove from his arm and reached for Mary's hand. He turned to look at her.

'Thank you, love,' he said. 'Thank you.'

Then, soon enough, it was milking time.

Branded

*K*rissy reached for the lever on the woolpress and jerked hard. The doors flew open and the wool bale emerged suddenly, with a bang from the pressure release. She grabbed a bale hook hanging from the side of the press and with a determined *thwack* pierced the wool pack and dragged it over onto its side. The bale thudded onto the wooden floor, rattling the old grimy windowpanes and shaking the corrugated-iron shed wall.

As Krissy stooped to write number fifty in the wool book, and record the bale's 150-kilogram weight, she smiled. Outside, she could hear the gorgeous Shaun letting the last of the off-shears wethers out of the footbath, hooves scuttling on concrete and Macca putting in one last deep bark for good measure. She pictured young Shaun, his checked blue shirt undone a fair way to reveal a baby-smooth chest flecked with soft dark hair, his curved eyelashes blinking long black curls out of his hazel eyes, and all the while looking country boy rough-and-ready-for-it in his lanolin-soaked John Deere cap.

He was a sweet lad. So sweet, Krissy thought wickedly, that this morning she hadn't been able to help sucking on his long, lively cock just before dawn and right when the cook's bell had sounded from the shearers' mess to tell them breakfast was ready.

Minja Downs was one of the few places that still ran live-in quarters for shearers, and every year Krissy loved the anticipation that she felt building inside her, knowing that she was headed there again to join the crew. In her younger days, Krissy had been the best woolclasser about. A born leader with the shed staff and, beyond that, sharp as a tack. She had had the ability to follow the trends in the international wool game and could class the wool accordingly as it came off the board, expertly sorting the fleeces into the bins so that the farmer would make the most money possible from her wool lines. After work, Krissy was always studying the agricultural papers and roaming through internet wool sites on her laptop, the keyboard of which was blackened by wool grease. The pint-sized energetic Krissy had been so passionate about sheds and sheep that all the cockys liked her and she was always in demand. At one point in her career, Krissy was travelling and working the sheds pretty much full time, with an eye to climbing the ladder and becoming a wool industry corporate. Offers kept coming in from the big players for her to work for them. There were overseas trips too, such as industry exchanges to New Zealand and England. The prizes that she won in the wool industry sports competitions had begun to fill her mother's kitchen dresser. She had a bright future.

But that was before Wayne Rodgerson, and before she had, stupidly, let her fanny run away with her dreams.

At the age of twenty-six she'd fallen for Wayne and promptly had three kids in three years to him. Her life as she'd known it had derailed entirely. For six years she and Wayne had shacked up together in a two-bedroom, rusty-roofed weatherboard shitheap on a so-called highway just out of Dubbo. God only knows, Krissy mused, why she had even been won over by the gun shearer Wayne and his smooth talk in the first place. She was smarter than him. She should have seen through him. Plus, he already had a certain reputation.

But her hormones had fired when she had felt the erotically charged air around him. She had lost her breath at the sexually attractive, masculine way he stooped over the rams while shearing, his pert arse upwards and his ice-blue eyes darting to her flirtatiously as she moved around the wool table, plucking the skirtings from the fleece before bundling it into the wool bins. Then she'd turn back to Wayne for another perve. His arms were to die for, rippling with muscle and softened by wool grease. And he was a bad, bad boy, who smelled of a heady concoction of cigarettes, booze, shearing sheds and soap. At the time, he was irresistible. Krissy sighed. Three weeks in one shed together was enough time and enough shagging for Krissy to think it was love. She should have known better. She should have listened to her mother.

The wedding had been a riot though, with Wayne's mates hiring not only a Harley, but also a big, ugly bulldog named Trevor for the day as a ring bearer. If it wasn't the classiest affair, it sure was a lot of fun. And it *had* been a happy marriage, thought Krissy … for about a week. Then the shit had hit the fan. Yes, she thought now, her mid-twenties hormones and her fanny had a lot to answer for.

This past couple of years since she and the kids had cleared out and left Wayne, the one place Krissy had gained back a little of her confidence and former self-esteem was here on Minja Downs. She was boss of the shed; Minja's exclusive woolclasser. So precious was their fine merino wool, the Thompson family practically paid Krissy double her usual rates to be here. Even the divorce, which left her skint, and the drain on her resources of full-time care of three kids, hadn't stopped her making the long journey east in her beat-up old Holden each year. Good on her crusty, cranky old mum for minding the little buggers, so she could have some time away.

Usually she would arrive at Minja Downs on dusk and, after a quick hello at the homestead with the Thompsons, head to the shearers' quarters where cookie was already on the job and on the grog. Then she'd drag her bags out of the car, dump them in the best room of the quarters, always reserved for the classer, and make her way over to the shearing shed. There she would stand quietly on the board, the only sounds were tomorrow's sheep milling about on the grating and the occasional bleat, and she would shut her eyes and inhale the scent of the place, thinking there was nothing like the smell of the shearing shed. Then she would picture how, tomorrow, the sleepy shed would be jolted awake with the arrival of the shearers. The tin would rattle with the buzz of machines, the daily business and brawn of men and the tumble of snow-white fleeces. The staff would catcall and larrikin it up, then there would be the lulls when the monotony kept everyone silent, engaged in their own mental battles within. There would be the occasional explosion of swearing brought on by the sudden kick of a sheep, or the occasional fleece that was booby-trapped with savage burrs. The running of the rouseabout, the clatter of hooves on flooring, the sudden kick of the handpiece as the shearers pulled the starter cord, was all evoked in her mind. The ebb and flow of a shearing was like a dance for Krissy, like a really good dream. Her long days cocooned in one team, in one shed, on one farm. Bonded with the crew, the hard days distracted the mind from its inner demons for a time.

For Krissy, Minja represented the ideal of her past life when she was a full-time classer; where she had always enjoyed a bit of fun, a lot of hard work and a beer in the evening with Trev and his crew. Nowadays it was her only shed and Minja took her out of her real life of dishes and washing-up, of breaking up fights between her kids, cajoling them to school each day, driving them all over the place amid the wastelands of suburbia. This year, with her youngest identified as having severe learning difficulties and her eldest almost expelled for behavioural problems, Krissy desperately wanted to be taken out of her always stressful, always mundane, life. She had been banking on Minja Downs to add a little spice, but not once in her dreaming of Minja Downs did Krissy ever bank on the spice of Shaun.

She and Shaun had 'happened' last night when she returned from her pilgrimage to the woolshed. After her meditation there, Krissy went back to the shearers' quarters peaceful and eager and, happily, found the rest of the team had arrived and were in the process of unloading their cars.

The men had greeted Krissy with backslaps and handshakes, introducing the board boy as 'newbie, shed virgin, Shaun the sheep'. It was only his first season in the sheds and Krissy almost rolled her eyes. She liked the board boy to be fully trained. Trev sensed her concerns and, as the contractor, added, 'But he learns quick, if you treat him right.'

Then the team, including Krissy, had got themselves full on cookie's first-night offerings of chops, mash, corn, peas and carrots and topped themselves up with a carton of Tooheys and a good dose of catch-up conversation. Eventually, as the fire in the mess dithered and began to die, one by one the shearing team had sauntered off to bed, winking at the new board boy, Shaun, wishing him luck getting to know 'the boss'.

Soon it was just her and him left, both sitting on the couch.

'I'm off to bed too,' Krissy had said, looking up at the bare light bulb that hung from a cord through the cracked, unpainted ceiling. 'Big first day tomorrow. Early start to get my bins and lines just right. And I expect my rousie to be on the ball, so you had better shove off too, Shaun.'

She narrowed her eyes at him as he fizzed the lid off the top of another stubby.

'Just the one nightcap,' Shaun said. 'Want to join me?'

Krissy sighed. 'You always pay for just one more,' she said, standing and putting another log on the fire. 'But … why the hell not?' she said as she sat on the couch again.

Reaching to the old tea chest before her that served as a coffee table, Krissy grabbed one of Shaun's beers, pulled it from the plastic, topped it, then swigged.

They sat in silence listening to the open fire snap, staring at the darting yellow flames that were livening up the blackened recess of the brick fireplace. She gradually realised his deep hazel eyes kept darting around to look at her and he was shuffling a little closer to her bit by bit. He gave her a sudden shy smile. She returned the smile.

Thinking back over the evening, Krissy had noted the many glances Shaun sent her way when the banter was running high between the crew. Then there was the brief brush of his hand as he passed her a beer, and the way he had sat with his thigh touching hers on the threadbare grimy couch. At first, Krissy thought Shaun had sat so close because of Dozer parking his massive arse alongside and shunting Shaun practically on top of her, the old couch threatening to buckle beneath the three of them. But Dozer was long gone to snore the roof off the place, and Shaun had had every opportunity to move away, but still he inched nearer to her. He was in such close proximity, Krissy could hear his Adam's apple glug up and down as he swallowed his beer in anxious gulps, as if he was gasping for air.

She narrowed her eyes again. She knew the blokes were up to something. They never went to bed this early on the first night. She twisted her mouth to the side and thought briefly before she suddenly twigged. Trev had laid a bet of some kind! He probably had fifty bucks riding on whether Shaun could bonk her before the week's end. As he was a newbie, they must've been giving 'Shaun the sheep' hell on the long drive out to Minja. Toying with him endlessly. Krissy realised Shaun would be going along with whatever Trev said just to fit in. That would explain the moves he was making on her. It would explain the sniggering between the men. The winks. The nudges. The 'goodnights' laced with innuendo.

Silly bastards, Krissy thought. And poor Shaun. She stood up and moved away, looking at him directly. Taking him in properly for the first time. He was hellishly good-looking and incredibly young. It made her rumble with anger at the older men. They could be such cruel buggers. But then again, Krissy thought, Shaun was a bit of a goat to go along with them. Where were his balls? He didn't have to be here now. She frowned at him.

He sat on the old brown couch, not knowing what to do or say, so he reached to the arm of the chair where Dozer had earlier jabbed a first-aid needle into the fabric. Krissy got the feeling he might be losing courage now that the rest of the team had gone and she was staring so openly at him. He suddenly bent his head and intently began trying to dig a thistle out of his index finger with the needle. Krissy looked down at him from where she stood, her back to the crackling fire.

'How much did they put on?' she said suddenly.

'Huh,' Shaun said, glancing up.

'In the bet.'

'What bet?' he asked.

She watched Shaun's cheeks flame red and the muscle in his square jaw clench. His Adam's apple danced again. This time he wasn't swallowing beer.

'How much?' Krissy pushed.

He shrugged.

She moved over and took the needle from him. 'Here,' she said, 'I'll do it.' She sat, clasping his hand, and began to dig into the pink pad of his fingertip. She felt him shift uncomfortably in his seat. She held his hand firmly.

'Was it fifty?' she asked.

He shook his head.

'A hundred bucks?'

He shook his head again.

'How much?' she urged.

'Twenty,' Shaun said quietly.

'*Twenty? Twenty bucks!*' She exploded with indignation. 'Is that all you offered to bet? Huh, you must think I'm easy. Bastards!'

The red blush on Shaun's cheeks was now running down his neck. He couldn't look her in the eye.

She turned to face him. 'And you'd do it for twenty?'

He squirmed again on the couch. Then his body jolted suddenly as she jabbed the needle in a little too hard.

'Ow!' he said, pulling away.

'Sorry,' she said. He glanced at her nervously as she grabbed his hand again, a grimace on her face.

'Taking a bet to sleep with the classer,' Krissy chastised. 'How can you lower yourself like that? A nice young man like you, being put up to it? What would your mother say?'

'It wasn't that they … we … thought you were easy,' he said, his head hanging down. 'They reckoned you'd had a bit of a dry spell, you know, with the divorce and all. They reckoned you'd had a hard time. And that I could make you happy. They told me you could be a mean boss in the shed if you weren't getting any. That I could improve your mood.'

Krissy pulled a face, her eyebrows shooting up. 'Did they now?' she said.

He nodded, grappled for his stubby and guzzled more beer. Then he set his beer down. He swallowed and turned to face her, settling his hazel eyes on her blue ones. He looked sincerely at her, his youthful face beautiful and unguarded.

'I don't see it as lowering myself,' he said quietly. 'When I first seen you, I thought you were a bit of alright. Bit of a cougar, really. Real nice. Real, real nice.' He bit his lower lip and lifted his eyebrows at her.

Krissy looked back at him. He was being sincere. She knew it.

'Oh, you poor, dumb darling,' she said. 'You should have picked up that Trev is a shit stirrer. You don't have to do what he says. No matter what.'

They sat for a time, Krissy holding the young rouseabout's hand as she continued trying to extract the thistle, their heads bowed close in silence. In the stillness, she felt an energy wrap around them. A melding of two lonely beings. Their breathing softened and fell into place together, in and out. Something charged the air. An anticipation. A longing.

'There you go,' she said at last, prickle removed, holding it on the pad of the index finger for him to inspect. He reached for her hand and moved it away a little, so his eyes could focus on what was a tiny, clear sliver of thistle.

'Amazing how much a *little prick* like that can hurt,' she said, her tone carrying meaning.

'Thanks,' Shaun said, guilt written on his face.

'Don't be sheepish, Shaun,' Krissy said, lifting his chin. 'We can all be made to look like suckers in this game. Bloody Trev. You really are a lamb, Shaun. This game can be tough and you need to grow up fast. I think they should call you Shaun the lamb, not Shaun the sheep. You haven't earned sheep status yet.'

Krissy caught a flash of irritation in his eyes.

'Cut it with the sheep jokes and my name,' he said with a flare of anger in his voice. 'I didn't plan on working in shearing sheds. I was at uni. Up until … Mum … she …' His voice trailed off. His jaw clenched, his mouth twisted in frustration. So, Krissy thought, Trev's stirring on the four-hour journey to the shed wasn't all he had endured.

'Died?' she finished for him.

Shaun nodded.

Krissy remembered what it was like to be twenty-one and new to the sheds with all that banter and stirring. She remembered what it was like when her dad had died. The aching void. She softened for Shaun and reached out and held his hand again.

'I'm sorry to hear that.'

He shrugged and his mouth worked a little, although he didn't pull his hand away. Instead, his thumb began to drift over the back of her hand, gently, in slow caresses.

He looked deep into her eyes. She smiled slowly.

'So, do you want to grow up fast, Shaun? Would you like to win twenty bucks off Trev?' Shaun's cheeks went bright red again, and his Adam's apple bobbed up and down. But he nodded emphatically and he was grinning at her cheekily.

She leaned towards him and they were kissing, at first softly, then with urgency, and then they were tiptoeing along the slanting hallway of the shearers' quarters, serenaded by the low rumble of snoring as they passed the closed doors, until they found themselves shut in Krissy's room. They tumbled together onto the sagging single bed where Krissy's swag was unrolled, waiting. The fog of chilled air came quick from their mouths as they hastily, hungrily, desperately, but delightfully, put their first fuck away.

Now, in the shed, Krissy heard the sliding door rattle open and shut as Shaun came in. She heard the sound of catching pens swing like saloon doors as he stepped onto the board. He stood looking at her in the dim light along the line of twelve shearing stands. He grinned as he walked towards her. As she stood over the bale, Krissy buried a victory smile and turned her back, reaching up for the wool stencils hanging on the wall from rusted eight-inch nails. He was gorgeous. A real looker. She was one lucky woman, and she knew there was plenty more to come. She placed the numbers' stencil onto the face of the bale and with the ink roller marked a blue five on the wool pack, followed by a zero immediately next to it. Then she grabbed for the Minja property stencil and inked it on, along with her professional woolclasser's number.

She heard his boots behind her and the tick of the corrugated-iron roof as the heat from the day dissipated into the blue sky above. She felt sweat trickle down her back and a warmth and wetness gather between her legs. Her pussy clutched in a wink of desire.

'Bale number fifty,' she said, her voice as soft as the fleeces within, 'SUP AAA FM — extra superfine — the best of the best and branded how I like it.' Krissy swiped a loose strand of her blonde hair away from her eyes. 'I've been waiting all day for this satisfaction. And this bale is *perfection*. That's why I don't like the woolpresser to do it. I wanted to press this one for myself.' Shaun smiled at her, his head tilted to one side like a curious, cheeky kelpie.

'I wondered why you sent Chugger back to quarters early when you had more pressing to do.' His eyes glinted in flirtation.

'You wondered right. Would you like a lesson in bale branding, young man?' she said, her voice loaded with invitation.

'I already know a little bit about it, but I'm sure you could teach me more, boss,' he said, moving to stand before her. Krissy could see from the bulge in his jeans he wanted more than a lesson from her. Close to him, she caught the scent of sheep and man's sweat. The faint drift of deodorant. Unlike last night, this afternoon, in this shed, Shaun seemed to have a new aura of maturity. A confidence shining out of him. As if he had stepped into a class of his own. He was quality.

She reached out, grabbed him by his leather belt and pulled him to her. Her breasts pushed upwards in her blue singlet, beaded with perspiration, wool grease sheening her skin and her nipples erect with wanting. She put her hands on his firm young chest and tilted her head as he bent and kissed her in a swirling energy of desire. Their tongues were sliding together, the deep French kisses gentle at first, although soon gaining the same frantic urgency they had had last night. Then Shaun kissed down her neck to her cleavage and she felt his hot breath and the scrape of his stubble on her skin as he slowly licked and kissed the gentle rise of her breasts, pulling her bra aside, his mouth finding her nipple. Starving for more, Krissy began to unbutton Shaun's shirt and peel it away from his angled, strong shoulders.

She breathed out a sigh of admiration at the perfection of his young body. His torso was long and smooth, tapering down to a narrow waist. Her desire was made deeper at seeing the change in him, no longer the shy boy of last night who had been almost crushed by the world. Today, he had been a man as he danced the dance of the shearing shed and offered her fleeces, tossing them lightly in the air so they drifted down onto the table with perfection. This budding man was beautiful, inside and out, and his mother would be proud. She felt a stirring of emotion, a need to nurture this man through this particular passage of time. She recognised the privilege that was hers in their coming together. The shedding of her old self and the remaking of the new. She pressed the palms of her hands against his skin, as if he was a god, and kissed him feverishly over his torso. Next, she tugged his belt buckle open and waited impatiently as he drew down his jeans, then kicked off his boots and socks.

'I want all of it off, now. I want you naked,' she said. Her eyes were locked on his, her blonde hair escaping more from its ponytail and falling over her face.

'Lie down,' she said, pointing to the bale. He obeyed. She gasped as she took in the divineness of his body spread before her, his cock rigid and pointing to the rafters, inviting her on for the ride. But not yet. She stooped over momentarily to breathe softly onto the head of his cock, making sure she didn't touch him. She wanted to tease him a little. She licked his cock once only, then blew again on it, hearing the deep inhalation of his breath and seeing the tensing of his stomach muscles, as his cock jumped in response.

She stood over him and popped the buttons on her Western shirt open all the way so her large breasts were better revealed to him in the blue singlet that she wore. His eyes fell to her breasts and she saw his cock jump and dance yet again. The head of it glistening invitingly. He began to move his hand along the shaft of his penis, but Krissy forced it away.

'No. No touching yourself. Just lie still,' she said. 'You are all mine.'

She reached for the branding roller and the AAA FM stencil. 'Like I said, the best of the best. Only the finest for me. And you, my dear boy, are a very fine specimen!' She set the stencil on his flat stomach and began to roll blue ink across it. He glanced down, a slight look of panic on his face, but desire pinned him there on the solid square bale. He dropped his head back and groaned a little. The ink smeared on his skin and caught in the little dark hairs that ran in a line down to the base of his cock. Krissy drew a finger along the line and then ran her hand up and over his cock. Easy does it, she thought, this one was young. She didn't want him going early, but he showed no signs. He was savouring it all, just as she was.

Drinking in the sight of him, she felt her pussy pulse with desire. Beautiful, inside and out. Quickly she shed her jeans and dragged her knickers down, dropping them on the lanolin-soaked floorboards, then swung her leg over him, straddling him backwards, propping her knees on the wool bale to better manoeuvre herself. She tipped her bottom in the air and dipped her head so she could wrap her lips around the head of his cock. He groaned as she slid her mouth wetly down over him and ran her hand up and down his stiff shaft. She angled her body and lowered herself, moaning as she felt his tongue flicker upwards to meet with her wet sex. He pushed his tongue into her and then ran it firmly over the taut button of her clitoris, as he used his long lean fingers to push inside her. The feeling of his mouth and hands was one of pure pleasure. She moaned and angled her hips further, so he could eat her more deeply, her breasts touching the blue pool of ink on his belly that was now smearing across both of them. His cock was sliding into her mouth.

Feeling the sensations he was creating between her legs with his mouth, she plunged her mouth over him even deeper, wanting to consume him. He was delicious and suddenly she *had* to have him inside her. With her lithe little body, Krissy spun around and faced him, her knees gripping solidly to the firm face of wool bale number fifty. As she lowered herself onto the tantalisingly stiff pole of his cock and began to tip her hips back and forwards, she watched as the juices from their bodies began to blend with the bale ink on his torso. With spread palms, Krissy smeared the blue over his stomach, her thighs and across her own belly, and laughed a little at the sight — it was like the face of Braveheart gone south. Then she let her full weight sink onto him so he was deep, deep within her. He moaned and breathed, 'Oh, god.'

Then, forgetting the world, Krissy began to buck and gallop and pitch, back and forth, riding him. Riding him hard. The heat and friction of the wool pack turned her knees red. Swathes of blue loosened by heat and mixing with sweat were smudged across their skin.

As Krissy felt her body rise to orgasm, she threw her head back. There, as she cried out, she caught a vision of wool draped over the beams looking like women's fine lace underwear tossed there without a care. As she gave one last thrust, her pussy spasmed in waves of orgasmic pleasure around Shaun's penis and she felt his fingers dig deep into the flesh of her thighs. His drawn-out cry of 'Ohhhh, yes' rose to the rafters as he came in shuddering spurts within her.

It was in that moment on bale fifty that Krissy felt utterly blessed by her life. This shearing shed was her church and, at this very moment, now, she worshipped this man. She could feel the divinity of skin on skin and the sacredness of the shared pace of their breath. They lay there for a time, his fingers drifting up and down over the goosebumped skin of her back, listening to the bleat of the sheep outside as the shorn mob walked onto water in the evening light.

Eventually Krissy sat up and smiled down at him. 'Shaun the ram, I reckon,' she said.

He grinned at her and reached to caress her breasts, her nipples still raised in desire.

'This will be the best twenty bucks I'll ever win,' Shaun said, smiling up at her.

'You reckon?'

Shaun laughed and nodded, then glanced down to his belly, his fingertips swiping at the blue bale ink.

'Does this stuff ever come off?' he asked, holding up a blue index finger.

'Not for a long while,' Krissy said, running her own ink-stained hands over his stomach. She could feel his cock starting to stir again inside her. 'So you, my beautiful boy, have just been branded. And now …' she grinned in good humour, '… Trev suddenly owes me fifty bucks!'

The Ride-on Serviceman

$\mathcal{E}$ dith Carter's property had the tidiest lawns of all the farmers' wives in the district. They were like the lawns of the royal estates back in England, ideal for croquet or strolling upon, but almost too refined for noisy, rambling children or summertime games of family cricket. The green swathe that was mown to perfection by Edith herself was irrigated almost daily with water diverted from her husband's farm dams. The lawns swept their way up to a grand homestead and seemed to announce to any who drove past the house that the Carters were from a very important dynasty of graziers.

The two-storey homestead was grandly constructed of stone and timber. At the front of the house, Iceberg roses climbed the verandah posts and bloomed prolifically in summer in resplendent white. The flowers were as pretty and delicate as fine tasteful French lingerie. Then there were Edith's box hedges, trimmed to perfection, curbing neatly around the white pebble driveway like miniature, elite show-jumping hedges for well-bred horses. The oasis of greenery, set in the heart of yellow fields of wheat stubble and dried pastures, was the focus of many garden club open days and country-style magazine feature articles and photo essays. The accompanying text in the magazines always proclaimed the Carters were indeed one of *the* most important grazing dynasties in Australia.

Never mind, mused Edith rather bitterly, that her husband's forebears had more likely stolen the land from its original inhabitants and that the true history of the Carter family was grubby, ugly and sordid. The place was tainted with forgotten and buried memories of shootings, beatings and rapings until the land was laid vacant and bare for the aristocratic Brits. The stylish articles never mentioned that bit, Edith thought. And no one seemed to think on it these days, nor mention it. Particularly the other women with whom Edith mixed. They had their tennis and book clubs, their mah jong and their trips to the city for 'a bit of a shop'.

Welcome to the world of the blissfully unaware, Edith thought. She wasn't judging them. She had been that way herself until her children had grown up, the last one gone to university a few years ago, and she now had the time to discover books. Not the ones the ladies read in their book club that were often covered in a shade of grey. But other types of books. Books on humanity, on history, on self-awareness, and lately, after the shock of Malcolm, books on sexuality.

If the Carters wanted to keep a patch of England alive against the western New South Wales heat, and live behind a facade, that was their choice. Facades were obviously their way. So, as a good grazier's wife, true to her husband's family facade traditions, Edith thought sarcastically, it was her calling, her charter, her duty as woman of the house, to keep a neatly mown exquisite green lawn. She didn't know why her husband complained about the water when it was his family's idea in the first place to design the garden just so. No amount of arguing from him, even in drought times, would keep Edith from having her lawn.

'You are overwatering!' he would shout.

'You are overgrazing!' she would shout back. 'I mulch my garden. Why don't you mulch your farm? Can't you see it's blowing away? Look at my garden soils compared to your cropping soils. Yours are dead. Mine are alive. You are a fool of a farmer. You are a fool of a man.'

'And you are a pathetic excuse for a woman!' he would shout again.

She would stand tall in her elegance and beauty, summoning every ounce of her dignity and strength, looking as regal and precise as Cate Blanchett even in her gardening clothes, and say quietly, 'You know, Malcolm, that garden is all that is left for my pleasure. *All that is left*. Would you deny me that too?' And her husband's eyes would slide away with shame and the matter would be closed for another few months, until water fell short again, or Malcolm announced he was going on another one of his 'ram buying trips' to the city, and then Edith would turn the sprinklers on flat out and the fighting would start up again.

Of course, as a woman, she had a right to be bitter. But she didn't want to think on that. Not today. It was such a splendid summer's day.

A perfect day to rid the roses of aphids and then jump on the mower for a run. It was even warm enough to find the excuse to have a midday gin and tonic with lime and lemon slices. And it was the perfect day for … *that*. She smiled and felt a wave of desire. She set down her pruning shears and adjusted her sunhat, glancing into the pretty gabled garden shed where the Cox 50 Farm Boss ride-on lawnmower was kept. Of course, none of the gardening club members, the magazine writers, nor her husband, suspected the real reason why Edith spent so much time in her garden and, in particular, mowing her lawns on the Cox 50. It was her own secret. And she was about to enjoy it now. Her own private facade. And one that had kept her relatively sane during the turmoil with Malcolm.

With her hands clasped around a giant glass of gin and tonic where moisture beaded on the rim and within, slivers of lemon and lime floated amid silver bubbles, Edith made her way to the shed. She listened to the drone of bees and summer flies busy with living high up in the leaves of the giant oak trees. She took another big gulp of gin and felt the ice-cold liquid enliven her mouth and throat as she opened the shed door and entered.

'Hello, Randy,' she said into the shadows. 'Have you been waiting long for me, darling?'

She drank again, then set the glass down on a potting table. 'Here I come, my gorgeous one.' She then swung a leg up and sat on Randy. She pushed his brake pedal in firmly, then turned the key. Instantly the vibrations shuddered through her. The wave of pleasure was instantaneous. 'Oh, hello! Randy, you good, good boy. I have so missed you since last week.'

She flicked the ride-on lawnmower into reverse and backed out of the garden shed, Randy revving loudly. She had found the thinner the fabric of her shorts or summer dresses, the better, the faster, the more frequent the pleasure on the Cox ride-on. Malcolm had often muttered that they should get the mower fixed, that it was not running right, never had. It shuddered and rattled and buzzed. But Edith had so far managed to distract him and the mower remained with its malfunctioning pleasurable vibrations. It had become her own movable, mowable machine of pleasure that she hid in the shed, not the bedroom drawer. She loved summertime.

For Edith, wintertime was not as much fun, not so much because her clothing was thicker and the sensation less intense, but because the grass slowed its growth and there was no excuse to mow.

But now, in summer, with the watering coming on each evening from fine, pop-up spray nozzles, Randy was needed often. The moisture and the sunshine meant the lawn was alive and thriving. And so too was Edith, with each juddering turn in front of the house.

She set the mower into gear, revved the throttle, dropped the blades lower with a clunk and then accelerated away, first to the right so the clippings were discharged away from her boxed hedges and the driveway, then she swooped to the left. With the blades set and spinning rapidly, a vortex of rattling encased the mower and shuddered through Edith's body. Her vagina suddenly engorged with wetness as she felt the sensations deep within. She shut her eyes momentarily, then turned her face to the sun and upped the revs. Juddering along, the pulse of the engine was translated into waves of sensation. Edith tipped her body forward and, with a deep gasp, quaked to her first orgasm. Gripping the steering wheel, she turned again, while the shivering pleasure tremored through her body. It was a quick one today. She put it down to the light linen dress in the pretty pale blue that she wore.

She could feel her sex deep within her quivering, and blood flowed up to her cheeks. It was a thrilling sensation. She was utterly addicted to her Cox.

She relaxed for a few passes, drew up the blades with a flick of the lever, and let Randy idle for a time as she stopped at the garden shed for another swig of gin. It was hot work. Then she hastily walked back to the kitchen for a quick refill, the feeling of her linen dress moving deliciously over her skin. From the verandah, she surveyed the yards and shearing shed and glanced across to the machinery shed. All was quiet. There were no workmen about. She could hear Randy's engine purring and whirring in the garden on idle, in neutral. Slugging more gin and tonic, she went back along the flagstone verandah, ducked under the climbing roses, swung up and climbed onto Randy again.

She revved him to seismic intensity and dropped the blades. The moment they engaged she felt their oscillation quivering through the seat, and within her the trembling of desire grew again in her groin. She swept the mower back onto the path. It had taken her some time to perfect the straight lines even in mid-orgasm, but Edith had the steering motion down pat. She headed down the hill towards the pretty pond. At speed, she could feel herself build and build with the thrill of the mower and was about to quaver to a climax when Randy gave a cough of his engine and died in a plume of smoke.

'No!' she cried out. 'Randy!' Edith leaped from the Cox and began to inspect the fuel, the lubrication of the parts, the oil, the battery terminals, but Randy was dead. She felt a panic grip her. He couldn't stop! Not now! She marched back up towards the house, grabbing her gin, and hurried inside. Hastily she clicked on the farm office computer in search of the nearest lawnmower servicing business. She typed in her postcode and waited.

There it was on the screen. *Hamish Redpath, your friendly local Cox serviceman.* Without delay, she called his number.

'Hello?' came a warm voice on the line.

'Hello, Edith Carter speaking. I have an emergency with my Cox.'

Two hours later Edith waited in the shade of the verandah for the serviceman, all the while looking longingly at Randy, who sat immobile and silent halfway down the gentle slope to the pond. Edith blinked tears out of her eyes and chewed sadly on a piece of rye biscuit. She had to eat something to soak up the gin. She knew in her heart she wasn't crying over a ride-on lawnmower. She was crying over the facade. The twenty-five year facade: of a marriage;

of raising children to a man who was a fake; of presenting prizes as Mr and Mrs Carter at the local show when everything had been a lie. The facade of a happily married couple. The wall of which had come crumbling down late one night when she had stumbled sleepily down the stairs in search of Malcolm.

Right from their wedding night they had slept in single, separate beds, cast apart from each other in the same room. The floor between them felt like a canyon void for Edith. Malcolm had set the rule, and as a young and beautiful, but very naive bride, Edith had obeyed. Malcolm abhorred physical closeness in bed. The night she found out why was so raw in her mind, the memory still twisted a knife into her as if the incident had happened last night.

But it had been three years since the crumbling of the facade, the night when Edith had walked the house like a ghost, in search of her husband. To this day, she wished she hadn't found him. Not like that. But there he had been, in the farm office, his back to her as he sat upon the office chair, his hand moving rapidly up and down in his lap. His focus was intense on the computer. The images on the screen … of men, naked. Two men, buffed and baby oiled, one behind the other, humping like beasts. Bumfucking while her husband of twenty-five years jerked off.

Edith had backed away, unseen, and gone to lie in her bed. Then the faded years tumbled to the forefront of her mind as she added up the signs. The lack of sex. The distance. The frequent trips to ram sales with very few rams bought. And the cruelty of men who couldn't tell their truths to women. The discovery had been her undoing. All these wasted years she had thought it was her. She wasn't desirable enough. She wasn't attractive enough. She was the boring one in the bedroom, so her husband never came near.

Edith, from that night, began to pay more attention to the records ... of phone bills, tax receipts, of internet trails to find proof so she knew it was true. And then she found it. Her life had unravelled via Google. She had it on the screen in front of her, in concrete proof with several receipts in her hand and a link to a gay bar in Sydney that hired out young men. As it all fell into place, Edith's world had fallen too.

For the past three years, it had been through the garden that she had revived herself. The life and death of nature helped to keep it in perspective. She would breathe in the scent of her gardenias and remind herself she was a proud woman. A good woman. She could cope with anything. Almost. However, there were days when the sordidness of her husband's deceit sat heavily on her mind and she found it hard to cope.

She had thought about taking snail bait or an overdose of pills herself. She had swamped herself in self-loathing. But then, always, she had thought of her children, off at university. How would it be for them? She had to find a way to live.

One day, Edith Carter, sitting on the lawnmower silently crying yet again over Malcolm's secret life, had discovered a way that she could overcome the mire of despair and devastation that she found herself in. With a phoenix-like fury, Edith had determined to lift herself up and hover above her world. She decided that day that she would not expose her husband's facade — she would defy it. And as she learned to tip her pelvis forward and rev the engine of the mower just right, she discovered within herself the power and the rampant drive of a wild sexual woman. So what if her awakening had come on a lawnmower? That mower had taught her to fly to the sky and back. Something Malcolm had never done. She giggled a little now. Malcolm's dirty secret was so much more predictable and boring: 'Married man secretly gay.'

'Yawn,' said Edith out loud. Hers was so much more lewd and thrilling. 'Mrs Malcolm Carter is having an affair with a lawnmower.'

Laughter spluttered up from Edith, just as the serviceman's ute rolled into her circular white pebble drive.

Hamish hopped out of his ute to see an elegant woman in a pretty, blue summer dress laughing to herself. He smoothed down his shirt and walked to her. Edith saw a handsome man in a smart pair of shorts and on the back of the truck a brand-new shiny red Cox.

'How lucky are you, Mrs Carter? The gods were smiling on you today. It's amazing I happened to be in the area. Rarely get out this way. But here I am!' He extended his hand. 'Hamish Redpath, your ride-on Cox serviceman.'

Edith took his hand and shook it warmly. '*Friendly* Cox serviceman! Call me Edith,' she said, taking in the neatly clipped grey hair that shone handsomely bright next to his outdoorsy skin tones of summer brown. He had green eyes, the same colour as her lawn, and his body was long and lean. Fit like a racehorse's form.

'So, you're the lady with the overexcessively vibrating Cox.'

'How did you know?' Edith said, unable to stop the guilty gesture of her hand flying to her throat and her cheeks colouring.

'Your husband comes in from time to time. He mentions it, but he never seems to bring the mower in for us to service. Shall we take a look?'

They walked in the summer sun towards the mower. Hamish lifted the bonnet and inspected what lay within. He um'd and ah'd a little as Edith folded her arms across her chest as if waiting for a diagnosis from a doctor about one of her children.

'It's an old model, Mrs Carter. A Cox 50. I've got one trick up my sleeve. If it works, he'll be up and revving, but if not, he may not be worth fixing. I've a new one on the back. Perhaps you'd like a demo? It's a beautiful unit.'

Edith shook her head. 'Please call me Edith. And no. I don't want a new one. I like this mower.'

'Okay. You're not the first person to get attached to their old Cox. But there comes a time when you have to let go of them.'

Edith nodded sadly and Hamish gave her a sympathetic pat on her arm. 'I'll get my toolbox, Edith.'

She watched the way his long legs ate up the distance between the mower and his truck, his boots landing solidly on the lawn. Nothing gay about that man's walk, she thought to herself, thinking of Malcolm and his lack of courage in everything. Hamish was honest. Edith could *feel* he was an honest man. Then she bit her lip. A Cox ride-on serviceman. It sounded idyllic. She didn't avert her eyes, nor disguise her admiration for him as he strode back towards her, toolbox in hand. He smiled back at her, equally as unashamed in his attraction to her.

'This may take a little time and tinkering, Edith. Why don't you take a seat?' He gestured to Randy's seat and took her hand, helping her on. His touch felt like the first drops of welcome rain on a parched landscape.

'Why thank you,' she said, squeezing his hand a little before he released his grip.

Hamish didn't miss the fact that she lifted her blue skirt quite high to sit astride the mower. He took in her nice, long, tanned legs. Still beautiful, she knew, for a woman of her age.

'Tell me, Hamish, are you single?' she said, curling a wisp of her fair hair around her index finger.

'As a matter of fact, I am. Divorced. Five years this summer.'

He opened up his toolbox and selected the items he needed. There was something definite and assured about the way he moved, she thought. He tinkered inside Randy, moving a small shifter this way and that. Then he took out a seal and blew on it a few times.

'It was the worst thing at the time. You see, my wife decided, quite late in life, she wanted to bat for the other team. If you know what I mean. She took off with the girls' music teacher, Ms Finnighan. So it's just me and the girls at home now. We manage and we're happy enough. Although I'm not much chop in helping them with the girlie things they need to learn. That's when it's hardest. They get a bit angry with their dad at times. I suppose it's only natural for girls that age.'

Edith listened and nodded, amazed at what she was hearing. She plucked at her dress and looked down at her lap.

'It's been the same for me,' Edith said. 'Malcolm, as it turns out, is just the same as your wife, although he hasn't been brave enough to leave.' She said the words quietly, but the relief in sharing the information about Malcolm, albeit briefly, felt like a shout to the stars. Edith felt the alleviation in pressure wash through her taut body. It was as if chains had snapped and a gateway had flung open. She now felt truly emancipated. It was time to move on, she realised. Now was the time.

Hamish glanced up sharply, unable to disguise the look of shock on his face. Mr Malcolm Carter? Then he hastily buried his shock and bit his bottom lip, and delivered her up a sad smile.

'I feel for you. It's crushing.' He blew out a breath. 'But each to their own,' he said, waving the shifter. 'It's healthiest if you don't see yourself as a victim. That you forgive and forget as best you can. But let me tell you, it's a shame people get hurt in the process of another not being honest about themselves. I guess it makes us look deep inside ourselves though … like we're looking into this here mower. You have to go within, under the bonnet, into the engine, to find the faults to fix. Same as ourselves.'

Edith nodded just as he set the engine cover of Randy down.

'Give him a go,' Hamish said cheerfully. 'See if that's done the trick.'

Edith felt a buzz of anticipation run through her as she began to turn the key. Randy gave one hopeful chug, but then fell silent. Hamish hmm'd thoughtfully.

'Please don't tell me he's done for,' Edith said, a frown creasing her high elegant brow.

Deep in thought, Hamish waggled his finger at her. 'Never give up, Edith. Never, ever give up. There's one other trick that can assist the starting mechanism to fire.'

Edith looked up at Hamish from where she sat on Randy, hope written on her face.

'This is one of the very first models to have an operator presence sensing switch, isn't it?'

Edith looked blankly at him.

'I'll explain … if you don't set the park brake and you get off the mower, the engine cuts out and stops, right? It's a safety feature.'

Edith nodded, not sure where Hamish's line of thinking was leading them.

'There's a sensor switch under the seat. Rider gets off, mower turns off. Got it? But this old man may have an issue with his switch. One of my little tricks is to add extra weight to the sensing switch. You're just a slip of a girl and the seat might need more weight. That factor, combined with a lifetime of heavy vibrational action, means the sensing switch may need recalibration back at the shop.'

The word 'vibrational' coming from Hamish's sexy, sincere mouth brought a flicker of desire to Edith. She wished he'd say the word again.

'So you can fix him?'

Hamish pulled a 'not so sure' face. 'We can test my theory by putting more weight on the seat, if you are in agreement?'

'I'll try anything!' said Edith.

'Okay. Hop off for a sec.' Edith obeyed and watched as Hamish flicked his lithe brown leg across the mower and sat upright on it. Gripping the steering wheel with lovely manly hands, he tried the engine. A slight tremor ran through the mower, but nothing else happened.

'More weight,' Hamish said. 'If you are game, you can sit on my lap. You are as light as a feather, Edith, but the extra kilos of both you and me combined could do the trick. The old boy will soon let us know if it's his sensor switch.'

She shrugged and opened her palms to the sky. 'I have nothing to lose, Hamish. Nothing at all to lose!' And with that she moved over to him, swung her leg across the mower and settled her bottom into his lap. She drank in the closeness of him. The smell of him. Lawn clippings and motor oil.

A flashback memory of her teenage years came tumbling into her mind. A summer's day at her Sydney boarding school. She the only boarder not allowed home for the weekend as her parents were abroad. Lying on her belly in a bikini out on the hot lawn, on a scratchy boarding-house blanket of grey with white stitching. The young man with the push mower coming ever so nearer, the rhythmic drone of the engine louder each pass. The glances between them. The small talk when the boy had helped her to move her book and blanket to a freshly mown patch so he could continue on with his work. The way he had raised one eyebrow and read the title of her book out loud.

'*Lady Chatterley's Lover,*' the beautiful mower boy had said. They had exchanged a glance and gentle smiles when they saw the school's housemistress disappear into her private residency, drawn away by a phone's shrill ring. The boy had come to sit beside her, leaving his mower idling so the mistress would not notice the suspicious silence.

'And how is your Lady Jane?' he said, eyeing her bikini bottoms, and with that question, Edith had lost all sense of herself. She and the boy had come together in a joining of mouths, a melding of sweat, a tangling of limbs and a sudden burst of adolescent summer heat. Sliding aside the crutch of her bikini bottoms, the boy had taken her. Edith's virginity blazed into the summer sky with a rushing of hormones more powerful than the pull of the moon. When they were done, she thanked the boy and caressed him down there and said tenderly, 'Thank you, John Thomas,' to his fading penis. Gently the boy had used the corner of the boarding-house blanket of coarse grey wool to swipe away the blood and semen from her inner thighs. Then he had pulled up his shorts and kissed her again, sweetly, on the lips.

'*Mow* we meet again,' she had said, and she and the boy had laughed.

Then the sun had gone behind a cloud, the housemistress reappeared, and the mower boy took the mower to its shed, packed up his things and left.

Now Edith sat with Hamish beneath her on the ride-on, her senses filled to the brim with the aromas of summer-cut grass and mower fumes, and smiled as she felt Hamish's hand move to her waist.

'Crank him over,' Hamish instructed. 'Give the old boy a go.'

Edith reached, turned the key and, with a solid rev, Randy fired up in an instant. Both of them whooped and Edith swivelled around to high-five Hamish.

'Told you!' Hamish yelled, his green eyes twinkling. 'But, jeez, he's got a bit much vibration in him!'

'I know,' said Edith with a big smile. 'That's what I like about him!' She delivered him the cheeky grin she had given the boy at boarding school. The sun was dipping now in the sky and casting a sweeping orange glow over the garden. Hamish took in the shine of Edith's even white teeth framed by her lovely smile, and the scent of her, moist and sweet like the fragrance of jasmine and moss, the undertones of her sex carrying a note he couldn't resist.

Beneath her pale blue dress, Edith could feel Hamish's erection nudging her buttock, while the resonating thrum of the mower continued to tremor and vibrate through both their bodies. She saw him resolutely reach for the park brake. She spun around, standing with her feet either side of the mower platform, her pointed nipples and her breasts almost brushing his face. She reached for the belt of his shorts and stooped to kiss him as she began to drag his shorts and underpants down, the thrum and zing of the mower and the smell of petrol fuelling her desire. She saw his erection, as if sculpted in beautiful pale pink, emerging from a tangle of male hair and she gasped.

Sliding her panties to one side, she sat directly onto his penis, her ready vagina taking him in easily. Together, joined, united, they felt the mower's quivering and wavering jolt through them. When Edith began to move her hips, the feeling of Hamish in her, along with Randy shuddering beneath them, was beyond the realms of her belief. She cried out above the noise of the mower in an instant orgasm that wavered on and on until she could bear it no longer. She had to lift herself up slightly from Hamish to relieve the sensitivity of her sex, so raw and on fire. Hamish held fast to her hips and began moving her up and down along the long pole of his cock, the shaft glistening in the sunlight. She cast her arms about his broad shoulders and plunged up and down, rocking, rolling, pounding on him as the buzz ran through them. Then she felt his hands press deep into the flesh of her buttocks and as he pulled her firmly onto his lap, he gave way with a throb and a shudder, spurting deep within her. Just as he did, Randy coughed and the engine shut down.

Edith settled her weight down upon Hamish, his penis still nicely hard inside her, and rested her head upon his shoulder, immersing herself in the silence and the stillness, save for their ragged breath and the song of magpies making ready for bed. She giggled a little.

'Has poor Randy died on us?'

'No,' Hamish said, his hands gently roving up either side of her back and beginning to massage her shoulders a little, 'he's just out of fuel.'

She laughed and pulled back from him, kissing him tenderly on the lips. 'Thank you,' she said.

'For what?'

'For really good service.'

'My pleasure, madam.'

'*Mow* we meet again,' she said and smiled at him a little sadly.

He laughed and kissed her lightly on her nose. 'Don't look so sad, Edith. We shall meet again. From the *mow*-ment I saw you, I knew I had to become your exclusive ride-on serviceman. Now, let's get this old boy onto my truck. I can deliver him back to you by ...' He paused, a cheeky look on his face. 'Let's see ... lunchtime tomorrow. If that suits?'

Edith had a quick think. Malcolm had a Rotary meeting in town. He'd be out until evening.

'Yes,' Edith said, 'that would be *mow*-st kind of you. I'll even have a nice bottle of *Mow*-selle chilled for us.'

'Really?' Hamish said with a wide handsome smile. 'That sounds *mow*-st fun!'

'And please, Hamish, if you wouldn't mind, don't worry about fixing the mower's vibrations this time. We can do that on your next service visit.'

'Of course, madam. I am at your service.'

Together they climbed from the lawnmower and walked hand in hand up to the garden shed in search of more fuel for Randy.

Look out for
RACHAEL TREASURE'S
new novel

The Farmer's Wife

IN APRIL 2013

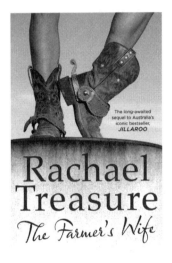

The long-awaited
sequel to Australia's
iconic bestseller,
JILLAROO

Rachael
Treasure
The Farmer's Wife

They got married and lived happily ever after ... or did they? *The Farmer's Wife* is the much anticipated sequel to the groundbreaking novel, *Jillaroo*. A beautiful and moving tale of self-discovery, it reveals the truth about relationships that the Cinderella stories never tell us.

Read on for an exclusive sneak peek at the opening chapters ...

Chapter One

'You told me it was a Tupperware party!'

Rebecca Lewis folded her arms across her chest as best she could with two shaggy terriers sitting on her lap. She scowled at Gabs, who was swinging on the wheel of the Cruiser like an army commando. Gabs aimed cigarette smoke towards the Landy's window and puffed out a cloud, then delivered a wide, wry smile from her unusually lip-glossed lips.

'Get over it.'

The women were lumping their way over the wheel-scarred track, once a quagmire during a severely wet winter, but now a summer-baked road of deep jolting ruts. As they wound their way over shallow creek crossings and valley-side rises, Rebecca shifted under the weight of Gabs's dogs and hunched her shoulders. She looked out at the dry bushland around them that ticked with insects in evening heat.

'I thought it would cheer you up,' Gabs offered.

'Cheer me up? Do I look like I need cheering up?' Rebecca frowned at her own reflection in the dusty side mirror. There were deep worry lines on her forehead.

Her blonde hair, dry and brittle on the ends, was carelessly caught up in a knot as if she was about to take a shower. Hair that looks as coarse as the terriers' fur, she thought. Bags of puffy skin sat beneath her blue eyes like tiny pillows. She prodded them with her cracked fingertips. Her mouth was turned down at the corners.

Could she actually be a bitter old woman at thirty-eight? She closed her eyes and told herself to breathe.

'How can you *not* be cheered up by that?' said Gabs, thrusting an invitation at her. Bec looked down to the silhouette of a woman naked save for her towering stilettos. The woman sported a tail and tiny horns like a weaner lamb. *Horny Little Devils*, the text read. *Making the world a Hornier place. Australia's Number One Party Plan.*

'Tupperware party, my arse,' Rebecca said, rolling her eyes.

The tiniest smirk found its way to her lips. She looked ahead on the road to Doreen and Dennis's farmhouse, tucked into the next valley. Maybe this party could be a turning point for me and Charlie, she thought hopefully. Ten years of marriage, two baby boys, the death of her father and a farm that failed to function. Charlie blaming the weather; Rebecca knowing different. Then there was her family, distant in the city. Her mother, Frankie, who seemed to not notice her, and big brother Mick, still treating her as if she was ten. And always, always, there was the memory of Tom. She sighed and pushed Amber and Muppet off her lap onto the floor and grabbed for Gabs's cigarettes.

Gabs glanced over with concern as Bec fumbled with the slim rolls of tobacco. Hands shaking, she put the smoke to her lips and swore as her thumb ineffectively ran over the coarse metal cog of the lighter, creating feeble sparks but no flame. She hadn't felt this down for years. Not since the years after her brother Tom's death.

'Oh, for god's sake!' she said, throwing the lighter on the dash and stuffing the cigarette back in the packet.

'Are you *right*? Since when did you take up smoking?'

Bec shrugged.

'Here,' said Gabs, passing her a bottle of Bundy, 'forget the ciggies, forget the cola. Just cut to the chase.'

'But we've got crutching and jetting tomorrow. And I've got to get the boys to the Saturday bush-nurse clinic. It's Dental Day,' she said, still taking the square bottle of rum from Gabs.

'Dental Day! Again? Thank god Ted doesn't have teeth yet and Kylie isn't due for a checkup for three months. C'mon, ya bloody sook! Listen to you!' Gabs made whining noises — a parody of the complaints that Rebecca repeatedly made, about Charlie, about the farm, about the weather.

'For god's sake, Bec, go have your period and jump in a shark tank! Life can suck: so what? Make the best of your lot.'

Rebecca looked out through the bushland towards a stand of white-trunked gums and cracked the yellow top off the bottle. From where she sat, Amber sniffed at the rum and wagged her feathery terrier tail.

'None for you,' Rebecca said gently. She swigged deeply and grimaced at the rawness of the alcohol on the back of her throat.

Gabs looked across at her, softening now. 'I know it's been tough, with the mixed-up seasons and … you know … but build a bridge, Bucket! You'll have fun tonight. And I didn't suck my tits dry with a pump for Ted's bottle just for you to pike out on me.'

Her friend's tone was humorous, but Bec wished it was harsh. She wanted a kick up the arse. She was used to harshness. She thought of Charlie again and the sight of his broad back as he'd slammed the door of the kitchen that afternoon, taking his fury with him into the yellow and green cab of the dual-wheel John Deere. She pictured him going round and round now in the dying light of the hot day, the big wheels crushing a track through the dust of the paddock. A paddock she'd begged him not to plough.

Once Rebecca had liked tractors, loved them in fact. And had loved Charlie within them. During the early summers of their marriage at Waters Meeting, she remembered the sweet smell of freshly baled hay. The big roundies bouncing out the back of the New Holland and rolling to a stop on the green summer meadows. The way the cab door'd open and Charlie would appear like a Bull Rush clothing catalogue sun-kissed god. His boots landing solidly on the steps of the cab, socks covered by canvas gators, the golden hair on his tanned legs covered in a fine film of dust. His teeth glistening white in the sun as he smiled, stooping to kiss her. She remembered him taking the smoko basket from her and dropping it into the fresh-cut pasture, and how he'd pressed her back up against the giant tractor wheel, kissing her harder, putting his strong hand up under her shirt, the smell of the hot sun on the rubber tyre making the moment even sexier. His hands urging between her legs, which were smooth and honey brown in ripped denim shorts. Summer love. Newlywed love. Tractor love.

Rebecca shook away the memory. Long gone now. The farm and the river that had run through it and fed her soul had dried up — and so had that magic between her and Charlie. Nothing seemed to lift her out of a stupor that had only deepened when her second son had arrived. Nothing, except for meeting Andrew Travis. After that her whole world had begun to shift. Everything felt changed. She crushed her back teeth together till her jaw ached.

'Maybe I should go on anti-depressants.'

Gabs butted out her cigarette in an already overflowing ashtray. 'Or maybe you should go on a ten-inch dildo!'

With the Bundy now starting to warm her, Rebecca couldn't stop a sudden jolt of laughter spluttering up, just as Muppet and Amber nosed their way back onto the seat and sat like a pair of Ugg boots back on her lap. Reaching over the dogs, she picked up the hot-pink Horny Little Devils catalogue from the dash and flicked through it.

'So what is a Jelly Butt Plug and a Gliterous-G anyway?' she asked, her head tilted quizzically to one side, her freckled nose wrinkled.

Gabs shrugged. 'Dunno, but I'm sure we're about to find out!' And with that she floored the LandCruiser, setting it sail over a culvert drain. They shrieked as the wheels spun mid-air. The Cruiser landed with a bone-jarring thud, tyres hitting the rims, smokes falling from the dash, dogs' claws digging into Bec's thighs, two-way radio handpiece falling down. Then on the women drove, their laughter drifting up to the sky along with the dust.

'Fuckerware party, here we come!' Rebecca yelled.

Chapter Two

Charlie Lewis took a swig on his stubby then set it down in the drink holder beside him, belching out a puff of beer-soaked breath. He adjusted the revs on the tractor, feeling smugly satisfied with his choice. Why should he settle for a 224-horsepower tractor when he could go all the way to the top with a 300-horsepower one? Plus, as he'd told Rebecca several times, he could get a bonus diesel voucher from the dealer if he bought it before the end of January. And it came with not just one but two free iPhones!

'One for the missus,' the dealer had said brightly.

Charlie checked his phone to see if he was in range. It'd be good to call Garry to have a bit of a skite about the new Deere.

There was better mobile service at the top of the riverside block so he'd have to wait another round to make the call. The digital clock in the tractor was glowing 8.36 p.m., exactly matching the time on his phone. He patted the tractor dash.

'Legend,' he said to it.

Garry, who had finished shearing at Clarksons' today, would by now be taking the cut-out party of his rouseabouts and shed hands to the Dingo Trapper Hotel.

Charlie wished he was going too, but he thought back to this afternoon and identified a foreboding conviction not to push his wife on the issue. She was still snaky with him for coming home at two in the morning after cricket training on Thursday.

Charlie remembered that afternoon in the kitchen, and the sight of Rebecca's jean-clad backside, which looked surprisingly broad from his angle, as she rummaged around in a cupboard.

'Why can't I find any fucking lids?' Rebecca'd said, jumbling through the clutter. 'No matter what I do there are never any complete sets. And why is every bloody party organised round here "bring a plate"? I don't know how many of my effing containers are scattered about the district! And now they want me to buy more at a bloody Tupperware party tonight! It does my head in.'

Charlie wanted to say, 'Everything does your head in these days.' Instead, he bit his tongue.

In her exasperation Rebecca began to crash things about a little too roughly for Charlie's liking. He knew the plastic container cupboard was dangerous territory. It was the place where he had seen his wife lose her shit the worst. Particularly when it was school bus time and Ben's lunch wasn't quite packed and ready to go. Best not to offer help at this stage, he thought, just in case. Charlie leaned on the bench, hands thrust deep in his pockets, looking down to the front of his blue checked flannelette shirt, where the buttons strained. He tried not to look at Bec, who was now kneeling on the floor holding a blue ice-cream container in her lap, staring at its lidless form. Her shoulders were hunched forward, shaking.

Oh, shit, Charlie thought, is she crying? Over lidless containers? Or is she laughing? He bit his lip and rolled his eyes, sauntering forward, knowing he'd have to do something now.

'C'mon, Bec, it'll do you good to go to Doreen's. You could get a new set of containers. Get a bit more organised. It'll help you spend less on groceries.'

Bec swivelled around and delivered him a flash of fury so strong it was like a kick to the head.

Charlie held up his hands as if surrendering to a firing squad. 'I was only trying to help.'

Bec got to her sock-clad feet. 'Help? You reckon help? Patronise me more like.'

'I ... I ...' he stammered.

'When the fuck did my life become all about Tupperware and messy cupboards, Charlie?' Tears welled in her sky-blue eyes, her face scrunched with emotional pain. She thrust the container violently at him and he received it like a mid-field rugby pass, clutching it to his stomach.

Charlie stared blankly at her, with his mouth open.

'What do I deserve that for? I work my arse off on *your* farm for *you*.'

'You just don't get it, do you?'

'What's there to get, Bec? You're always mad. You're always sad. Not much I can do about it.'

'Do you ever wonder *why*?'

Charlie shrugged.

'Maybe it could be something to do with a $200,000 tractor we can't afford,' Bec said. 'Jeez, Charlie! A tractor we didn't need. And then you went and got a brand-new fucking plough. And the fact that I'm stuck here! Stuck in this fucking house!'

'Someone's gotta do the house stuff. And you might think we don't need the machinery, but I do!'

'Why does the house stuff have to be done by me? That was never the deal! And you know how I feel about ploughing. Have you not listened to a word I've said on soils and no-till cropping? Since learning Andrew's stuff, I never wanted to plough a patch of dirt again on this place!'

Charlie, who had tolerated her surly mood till now, turned his head to one side and shut his eyes for a moment. Then he opened his eyes, glaring at her. The anger rose. 'Oh, yes! That's right! Andrew, Andrew, Andrew … your god of agricultural change!' he said sarcastically. 'Just because I'm not into your bloody new-age farming guff, don't take it out on me! You're just upping me because you like bollocking the crap out of me over nothing.'

'That's not true!'

Charlie thrust the ice-cream container back at her. 'Put a lid on it, Rebecca,' he spat. 'Find another babysitter for the boys. I'm going ploughing.'

Then he had turned and walked out, slamming the door.

Now, in the dying light of the evening, crows with wings like vampire cloaks were haunting the plough, trawling the clods of earth for grubs and arguing with the white cockatoos, who screeched and flapped with indignation at their dark companions. Charlie sighed and glanced at his green eyes in the rear-vision mirror, noticing the lines around the edges of them and the way his once-thick brown hair was now thinning on either side of his forehead. Where had the years gone?

And why did his time feel so wasted here? Here on a farm that had never been his. Waters Meeting. Rebecca's place.

He ran his grease-stained fingertips over his rotund belly and scratched it through the fabric of his bluey singlet. So what if he had a bit of a gut? What was the harm in a few beers? He thought of Rebecca and the way she constantly badgered him on his diet too, while she dished up salad for the kids that she had grown in her vegetable garden. He would glower at her and defiantly toss shoestring chips from a plastic bag into the deep fryer, along with a handful of dim sims.

'What's wrong with only wanting to eat peas, corn, carrots and spuds?' he asked one night as he pushed aside her dish of cauliflower cheese.

'The boys,' she said. 'Eating all types of good food is the most important thing for them to learn at this stage.'

He twisted the lid off a Coke bottle, relishing the loud fizzing sound, and eyed her as he gulped straight from the bottle.

She rolled her eyes in anger and turned away. She was so easy to bait like that. But bugger her, he thought. She could be so fucking self-righteous about everything.

For the first few years of their marriage it had been fun, and it was never about the fact that he ate mostly meat and spuds with a small side of peas, corn and carrots. She'd not minded then. She'd been a good chick and their days at Agricultural College had cemented their relationship into one of deep friendship. When he first moved to Waters

Meeting, he'd felt a sense of relief that he'd escaped his own family tangles on their farm out west.

After Bec and he were married, Bec's father, Harry, had been an alright sort of a fella to share the space of the farm with. One-armed since a post-digger accident, the old man had mostly kept out of Charlie's way, badgering Rebecca about what should or shouldn't happen on the farm. For the last few years Harry'd been too sick to do much anyway and stuck to himself in his log cabin. But since he'd died, Charlie had noticed a shift in Rebecca. A restless frustration. Some days her moods were too much to bear.

Then bloody Andrew Travis and his no-till cropping ideas and holistic grazing management seminars had got into Rebecca's head and she had completely gone off the dial about how he should run the place from now on. She was chucking out over ten years of his good management all because of some Queensland guru who kept banging on about regenerative agriculture and all the profits to be gained from low inputs.

Even though Charlie knew there wasn't much profit at the end of the day on Waters Meeting, couldn't Bec see their *production* was better than the other farms in the district? He remembered their shared passion in the early days when she'd brought him in as 'cropping manager' and, of course, her boyfriend.

For the first few years the business had hummed, exporting hay that was cut from the rich lucerne flats and shipped to fancy stables in Japan. They'd even travelled to Tokyo for a month, living it up with fancy-pants racing people who couldn't speak a word of 'Engrish' but could chuck back sake like you wouldn't believe. But five years into the venture the Aussie government had pulled the pin on water rights due to salinity issues hundreds of kilometres downstream from the farm. Charlie knew it had been more likely due to political pressures after a documentary screened on prime-time television about the evils of irrigation. The water was shut off to them. Waters Meeting had become a dryland farming operation overnight. And once again they had had to fight to keep the farm afloat.

In the midst of the fight over water rights, Rebecca had fallen pregnant and she'd become annoyingly philosophical about their situation, saying the irrigation ban was 'meant to be'. She'd said over time she'd realised that it didn't sit well with her to be carting hay around the world. It wasn't environmentally sound, she'd said. Bloody women always changing their minds, Charlie thought angrily. They'd bust their guts to set the operation up and now his very own wife was turning green on him like the rest of the wankers on the planet. What was wrong with her? Didn't people realise farmers fed the nation? And so they should be supported accordingly?

Charlie glanced again in the mirror and watched the plough discs cut neat crumbling lines in the dry paddock he'd sprayed a few days earlier.

A plume of topsoil eddied in the gentle breeze. He twisted his mouth to the side. It was too dry to be cultivating: Bec was right. There was something in his gut that told him what he was doing was wrong, but he just couldn't help himself. Kicking up dust was better than sitting at home watching Ben and Archie fight. He felt a twinge of guilt, knowing how crapped-off the boys would have been when they found out they were being plonked with Mrs Newton, their elderly neighbour, again for the night. They could've easily fitted in the spacious new cab with him. They'd been so excited about the new tractor.

Charlie swigged his beer and washed away the thoughts, instead choosing to focus on the new dream tractor. He loved everything about it, from the way the giant glass door pulled open, to the wide view from the cab through even more expansive glass. The massive John Deere was so sleek and modern it looked as if it belonged in one of Ben's Star Wars animations. It didn't just have a dash; it had a 'command centre display'. There was even a gyroscope that automatically made steering adjustments when Charlie drove fast down the smoother gravel roads of Waters Meeting. He'd love to try it on the newly sealed main road. Plus the GPS, once he'd worked out how to use it, would mean that his furrows would be perfectly even and straight.

He reached for his fourth stubby of the afternoon and popped the top off it, enjoying the gentle bounce the hydraulically sprung seat offered. It's enough to give me a hard-on, he thought wickedly, toasting himself in the mirror and cocking an eyebrow.

As he rounded up to the top of the paddock, his phone beeped a message. Garry, texting to say it was humming at the Fur Trapper, the locals' nickname for the Dingo Trapper pub. Charlie sent a text back saying he was on the chain for the night. Cranky wife. But bloody nice tractor.

As the sun dipped, and the fifth beer sank, Charlie settled into feeling a strange mix of boredom and friskiness at the same time. As if on cue, his phone beeped again with a text. He reached into his top pocket.

When he opened the photo up on his phone, he smiled and chuckled. There, on the small screen, was the image of Janine Turner in some rare kind of silky purple number with what looked like a black salami thrusting up from her ample cleavage. *Come get me later, cowboy!* came the message.

Charlie Lewis drained the last of his stubby. He paused for a moment. Knowing he shouldn't, but with the blandness of his life pushing him on, he reached for his belt buckle with a wicked grin on his face. What was wrong with a little bit of play? Janine was always up for it. She was about to get a nice shot of his gear stick. That would fix her.